WARNING:

This journal contains
wacky humor,
thrilling action,
nail-biting suspense,
cool raps,
and a mind-blowing cliffhanger!

Also by
RACHEL RENÉE RUSSELL

the misadventures of MAX CRUMBLY

LOCKER HERO

BOOK ONE

RACHEL RENÉE RUSSELL

with Nikki Russell and Erin Russell

ALADDIN

NEW YORK LONDON TORONTO SYDNEY NEW DELHI

ALADDIN * An imprint of Simon & Schuster Children's Publishing Division

1230 Avenue of the Americas, New York, NY 10020 * First Aladdin hardcover edition June 2016 *

Copyright © 2016 by Rachel Renée Russell * All rights reserved, including the right of reproduction

in whole or in part in any form. * ALADDIN is a trademark of Simon & Schuster, Inc., and related

logo is a registered trademark of Simon & Schuster, Inc. * For information about special

discounts for bulk purchases, please contact Simon & Schuster Special Sales at 1-866-506-1949 or

business@simonandschuster.com. * The Simon & Schuster Speakers Bureau can bring authors to your

live event. For more information or to book an event contact the Simon & Schuster Speakers Bureau at

1-866-248-3049 or visit our website at www.simonspeakers.com. * Book designed by Karin Paprocki *

The text of this book was set in Italo Medium Extended. * Manufactured in the United States of

America 0817 FFG * 10 9 8 7   * Library of Congress Control Number 2016904103 *

ISBN 978-1-4814-6001-9 (hc) * ISBN 978-1-4814-6002-6 (eBook)

To the original Max Crumbly, my nephew Preston,
a superhero with a magnetic smile,
ready to save the day with his signature karate chop
and his trusty sidekick, Chase the Dog

THE MISADVENTURES OF MAX CRUMBLY
(IMPORTANT STUFF YOU NEED TO KNOW IN THE EVENT OF MY MYSTERIOUS DISAPPEARANCE)

1. MY SECRET LIFE AS A SUPER~~HERO~~ ZERO

If I had SUPERPOWERS, life in middle school wouldn't be quite so CRUDDY.

Hey, I'd NEVER miss the stupid bus again, because I'd just FLY to school! . . .

AWESOME, right? That would pretty much make ME the COOLEST kid at my school!

But I'll let you in on a secret. Getting bombed by an angry bird is NOT cool. It's just . . . NASTY!!

TV, comic books, and movies make all this superhero stuff look SO easy. But it ISN'T! So don't believe the HYPE.

You CAN'T get superpowers by hanging out in a laboratory, mixing up colorful, glowing liquids that you simply DRINK. . . .

MWA-HA-HA-HAAA!

ME, MIXING UP A YUMMY
SUPERPOWER SMOOTHIE

HOW do I know it doesn't work? . . .

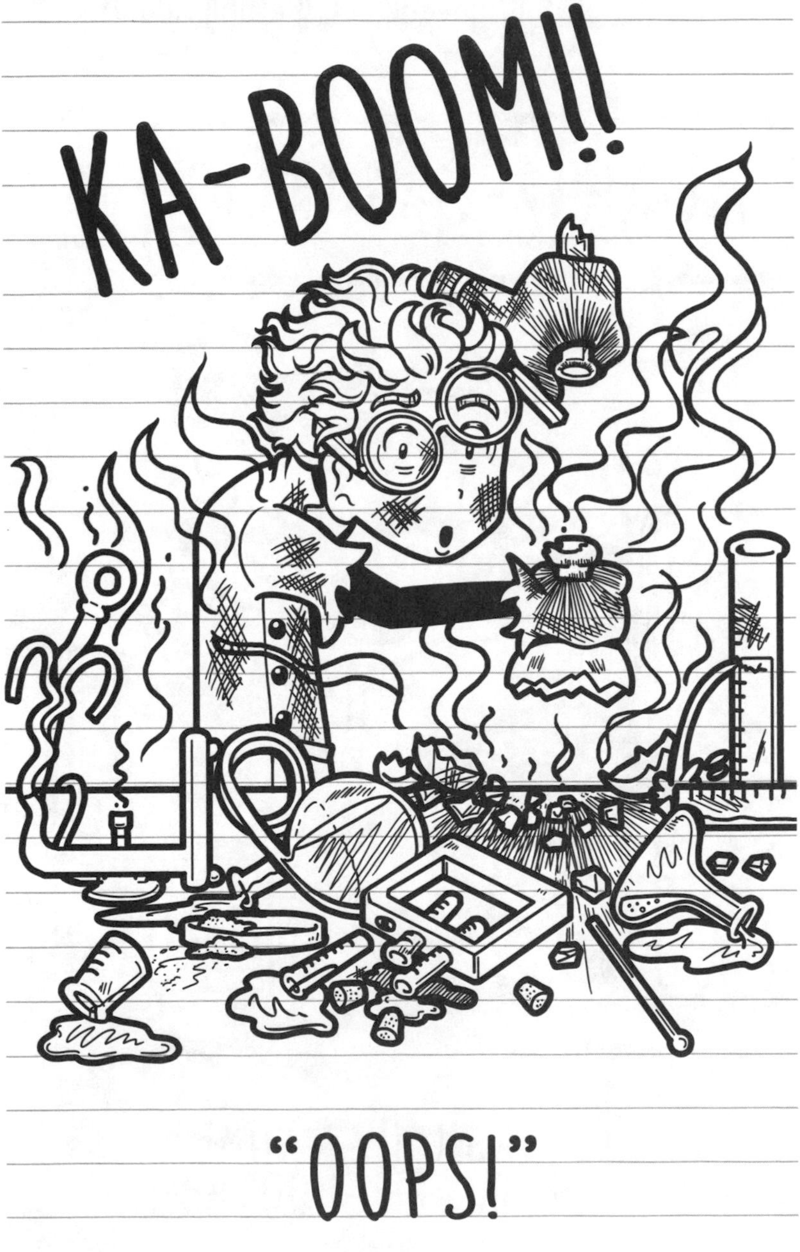
KA-BOOM!!

"OOPS!"

Let me put it this way. . . .

BEEN THERE. DONE THAT.
GOT THE T-SHIRT!!

Even if I DID have superpowers, the very first person I'd need to rescue is . . .

MYSELF!

WHY?

Because a guy at school pulled a lousy PRANK on me.

And, unfortunately, I might be DEAD by the time you read this!

Yes, I said "DEAD."

Okay, I'll admit that he didn't MEAN to kill me.

But still . . . !!

So if you're the type who gets FREAKED OUT over this kind of stuff (or comic book cliffhangers), you probably shouldn't read my journal. . . .

Um . . . excuse me, but are you STILL reading?!

Okay, fine! Go right ahead.

Just don't say I didn't warn you!

2. IF THERE'S A DEAD BODY INSIDE MY LOCKER, IT'S PROBABLY ME!

It all started as a normal, boring, CRUMMY day in my abnormally boring, CRUMMY life.

My morning was a disaster because I overslept. Then it went straight downhill from there.

I completely lost track of time at breakfast while reading a really old comic book that my father found in the attic a few days ago.

He said his dad had given it to him as a birthday gift when he was a kid.

He warned me to be super careful with it and not take it out of the house because it was a collectible and probably worth a few hundred dollars.

My dad was pretty serious about it because he'd already scheduled an appointment to get it appraised at the local comic book store.

However, since I was running late for school, I decided to ~~sneak~~ take the comic book with me and finish reading it during lunch.

Like, what could happen to it at school?!

Anyway, as I rushed to the bus stop, the zipper broke on my backpack and all my stuff fell out, including Dad's comic book.

I was like, Oh, CRUD!! My dad is going to STRANGLE ME if I damage his comic book!

I grabbed the comic book and was desperately trying to pick up everything else when the bus pulled up, screeched to a halt, waited all of three seconds, and then zoomed off again.

Without me!

Hey, I ran after that thing like it was a $100 bill blowing in the wind!

"STOP!! STOP!! STOOOOP!" I yelled.

But it didn't.

Which meant I missed the bus, was forced to walk to school, and arrived twenty minutes late.

Next I got chewed out by the office secretary. She gave me a tardy slip and then threatened an after-school detention because I had interrupted her while she was eating a jelly doughnut.

And just when I thought things couldn't possibly get ANY worse, they did.

When I stopped by my locker to get my books, suddenly everything went DARK.

That's when I realized I was TRAPPED in my worst . . .

NIGHTMARE!

I knew attending a new middle school was going to be tough, but this is INSANE.

My life STINKS!

I know you're probably thinking, Dude, just chill! Everybody has a BAD day at school.

Stop whining and GET OVER IT!

For real?

Are you serious?

Like, HOW am I supposed to get over THIS?! . . .

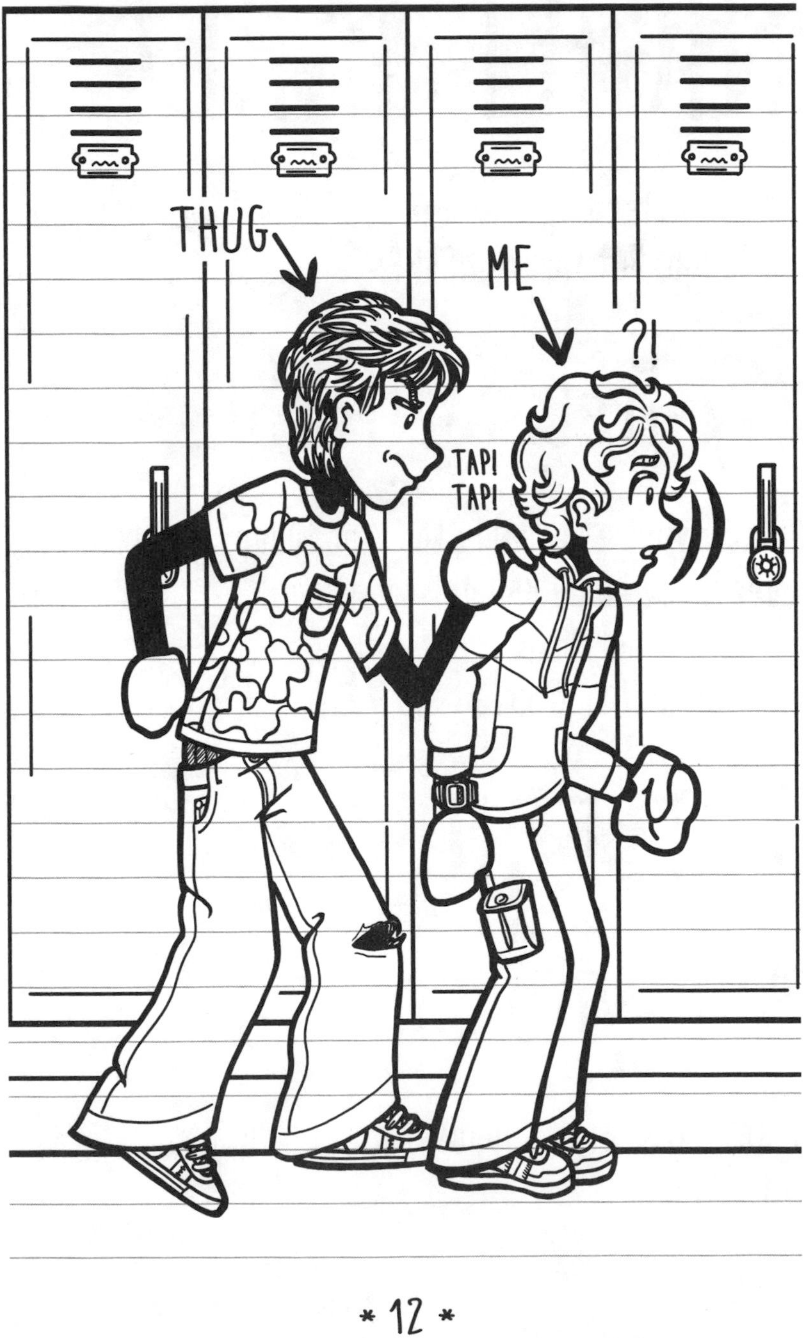
THUG
ME
?!
TAP!
TAP!

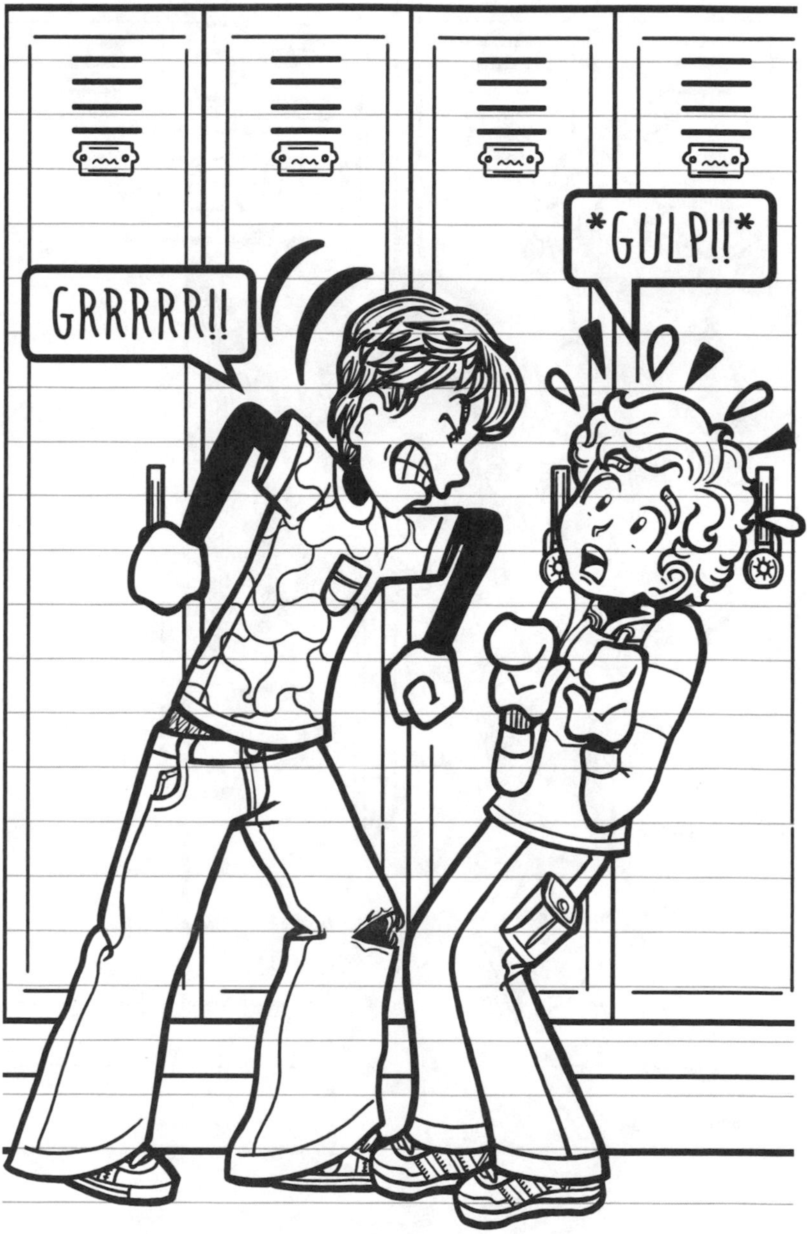
GRRRRRR!!
GULP!!

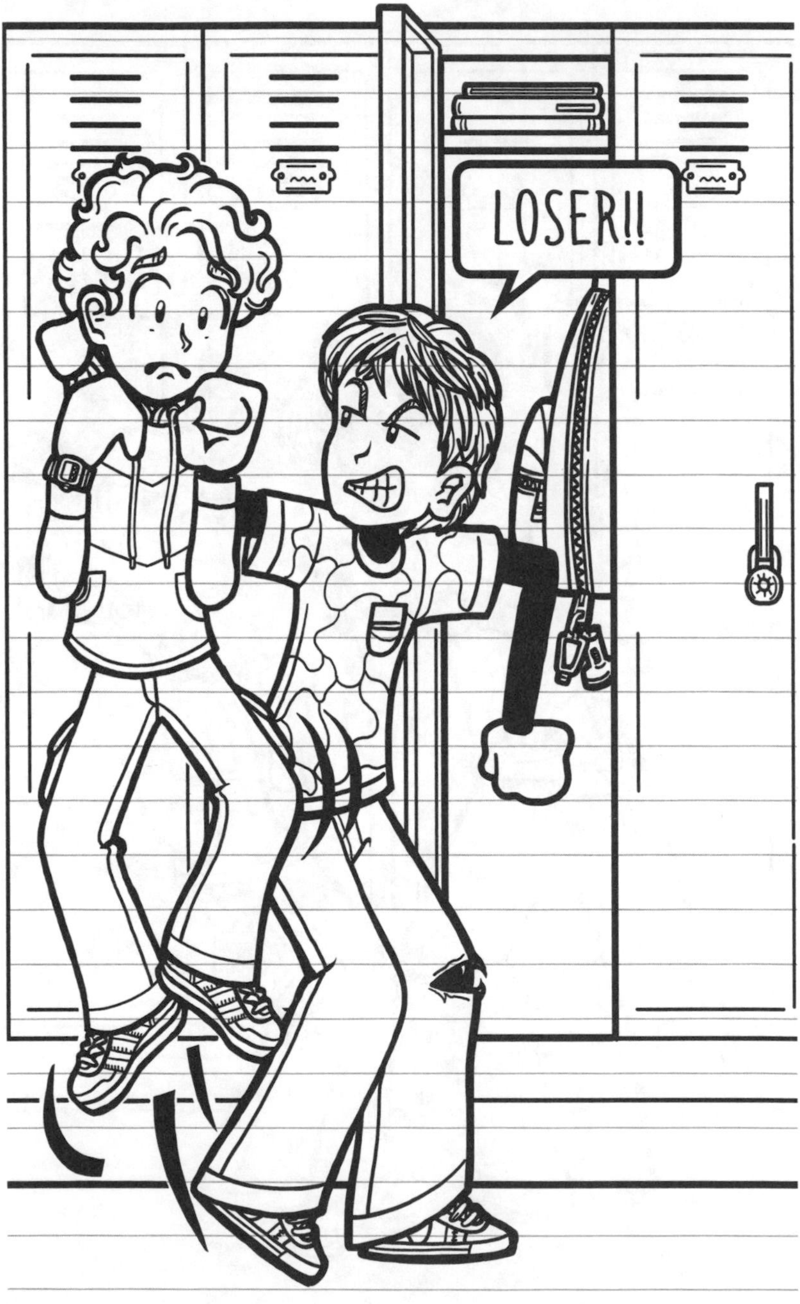
LOSER!!

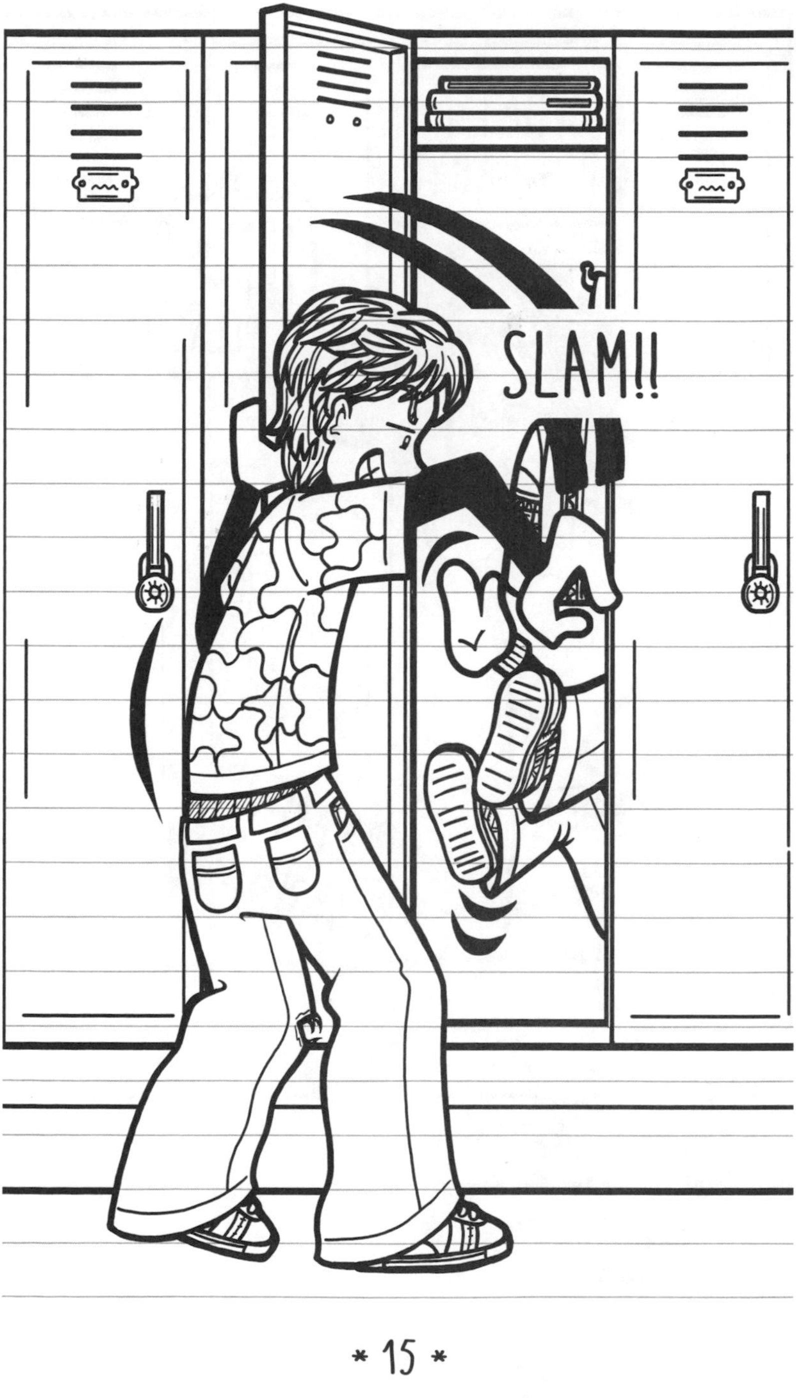
SLAM!!

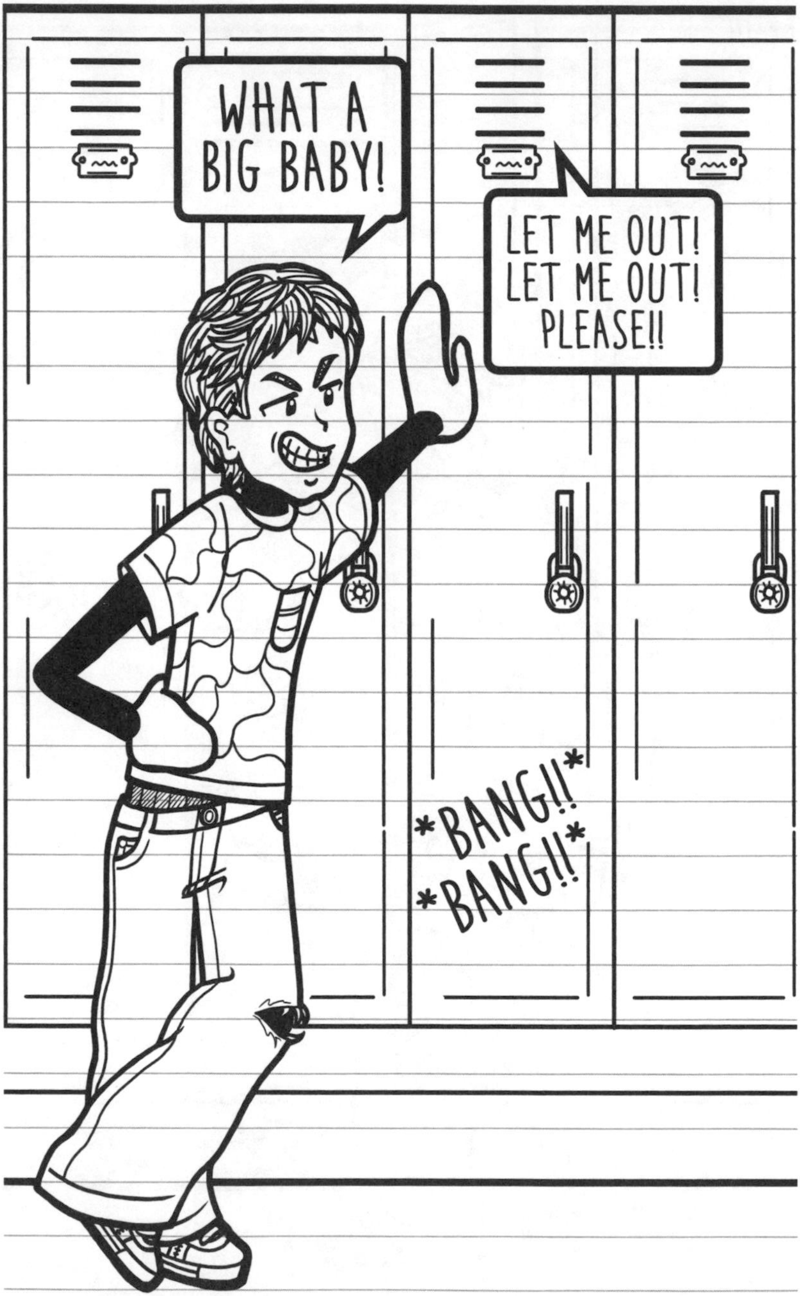
WHAT A BIG BABY!
LET ME OUT! LET ME OUT! PLEASE!!
BANG!!
BANG!!

Doug Thurston, better known as "Thug" Thurston, just STUFFED ME INSIDE MY LOCKER!! AGAIN! And it's only the second week of school.

Are we having FUN yet? I've been crammed inside here for what seems like forever!!

And, unfortunately, I don't have my cell phone to call for help! I was in such a big rush this morning, I left it sitting right on the table after breakfast.

My legs are so numb, I could probably saw off my big toe with my metal ruler and not feel a thing. And did I mention that I just had an asthma attack? If I didn't always have my inhaler with me at school, I'd probably already be dead by now!

I'm definitely going to be dead by lunchtime due to suffocation from limited oxygen and the stench of the funky gym clothes in the locker next door.

Which is ironic when you think about it, because I should have died DURING lunch the first time I ate the SEWER SLUDGE they try to pass off as food in the cafeteria!

~~And if all of THIS isn't enough TORTURE, I have to PEE! REALLY bad!~~

I need to figure out how I'm going to get out of this stupid locker.

Luckily, I have my flashlight key chain with me. Otherwise it would be pitch-black in here.

The ONLY reason I'm writing all of this in my journal is because I'm worried that one day Thug Thurston will stuff me in my locker and I'll NEVER get out.

So I came up with an ingenious plan.

When the authorities arrive to investigate my mysterious disappearance, the FIRST thing they're going to find inside my locker ~~(after my DECOMPOSED BODY!)~~ is this journal! . . .

ME, AFTER I'M FOUND INSIDE MY
LOCKER WITH MY JOURNAL!

I'm calling it THE MISADVENTURES OF MAX CRUMBLY, and it's basically a highly detailed record of all ~~the CRAP I've had to deal with!~~ my experiences here at this school.

Since there's a chance I WON'T make it out of my locker alive, I've provided enough evidence in these pages to send Thug Thurston away to PRISON!

For LIFE!

Or at least land his butt in after-school detention every day until he graduates ~~or drops out of school, whichever comes first~~!

Hey, I'm NOT trying to save the world or be a hero or anything like that, so don't get it twisted.

But if I can prevent what happened to ME from happening to YOU or another kid, then every second I spend suffering inside my locker will be worth it.

3. HOW DARTH VADER BECAME MY FATHER

I know some of you are probably thinking . . .

Is this guy for real? Is he actually writing all of this from INSIDE his LOCKER?

I totally understand and appreciate your skepticism.

I'M having a REALLY hard time believing all of this is actually happening to me TOO! I guess I should start by introducing myself.

My name is Maxwell Crumbly, and I'm an eighth grader at South Ridge Middle School.

But most of the kids at my school just call me ~~Barf, after I threw up my oatmeal in PE class~~ Max.

And YES! I did all these drawings myself.

Here's what I look like right now. . . .

Actually, that is probably NOT the best drawing of me. So let me try this again.

Okay, here's one that's a lot better. . . .

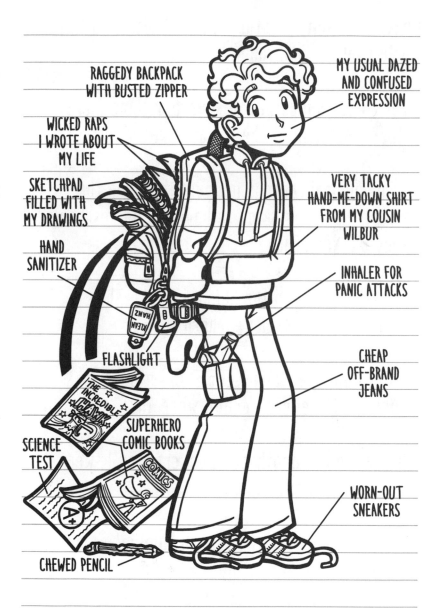

RAGGEDY BACKPACK WITH BUSTED ZIPPER

MY USUAL DAZED AND CONFUSED EXPRESSION

WICKED RAPS I WROTE ABOUT MY LIFE

SKETCHPAD FILLED WITH MY DRAWINGS

VERY TACKY HAND-ME-DOWN SHIRT FROM MY COUSIN WILBUR

HAND SANITIZER

INHALER FOR PANIC ATTACKS

FLASHLIGHT

CHEAP OFF-BRAND JEANS

SCIENCE TEST

SUPERHERO COMIC BOOKS

WORN-OUT SNEAKERS

CHEWED PENCIL

SELF-PORTRAIT OF ME (MAX CRUMBLY)

I have to admit, I'm still trying to adjust to this whole public school thing.

When I was younger, I had severe asthma and panic attacks, and one of the triggers was stress.

So for medical reasons my parents made the decision eight years ago to have me homeschooled by my GRANDMOTHER.

But that's not even the SCARIEST part. She's a retired KINDERGARTEN teacher!!

All the naptimes, sippy cups, and storybooks I endured in seventh grade were just . . . WRONG!

If I have to eat another animal cracker, I swear I'm gonna puke an entire ZOO!

Sorry, but there's only so much humiliation a kid can take.

So I secretly made plans to call Child Protective Services and report my grandma for CHILD ABUSE!

It was probably the happiest day of my life when my parents FINALLY agreed to let me attend South Ridge Middle School.

Since I'm a lot older now and on new medication, my doctor said I should be just fine.

The only complication is that if my parents find out I'm having any problem WHATSOEVER at my new school that could be stressful for me, ~~I'm gonna be stuck with Grandma, sippy cups, and naptimes until high school graduation!~~ they're going to snatch me out of this school so fast it'll make my head spin.

So I really need to fix this Thug Thurston problem. And FAST!!!

But it's kind of complicated because he's as big as an ox and kind of smells like one too.

I sit right behind him in math class, and some days it's hard for me to breathe. So I just plug my nose and mutter to myself. . . .

ME, TRYING NOT TO BREATHE THUG'S
TOXIC BODY ODOR FUMES

Do you remember me mentioning that I have an inhaler? It provides a strong dose of medicine to help me breathe.

Well, that thing is totally USELESS against Thug!

I scrounged around our garage until I found my dad's gas mask (his hobby is painting cars). And now I wear it to class for "medical reasons" whenever Thug's STINK is abnormally PUNGENT. . . .

← ME, WEARING A GAS MASK TO CLASS

The weird thing is that Thug is really friendly to me on the days that I wear it.

WHY?

Because he actually thinks I'm DARTH VADER'S SON! I swear. I am NOT lying to you.

He told me that when he grows up he wants to go to college to become a Dark Sith Lord just like my DAD. And he said he's already saved up $3.94 toward buying a black cape, a mask, and a red lightsaber.

Definitely some CRAZY stuff, right? But it makes sense when you consider the fact that Thug has flunked eighth grade, like, THREE times!

I almost fell out of my chair when he invited ~~Darth Vader's son~~ ME over to his house for pizza and video games.

But I decided NOT to go, because at some point I was going to have to take off my mask to eat a few slices of pizza.

And when Thug FINALLY figured out I really WASN'T Darth Vader's son, he was going to beat my face into a pulp.

If I could stand to wear that mask the entire school day, I bet Thug and I could become BEST BUDS!...

THUG AND ME, HANGING OUT!

Since we're on the subject of best buds, I can count the number of friends I have ~~on one hand~~ with just one finger.

A few weeks ago I met this guy at the store Pets-N-Stuff, but he goes to Westchester Country Day Middle School. I was there buying dog food with my grandma's crazy Yorkie, Creampuff, when the little furball started yip-yapping viciously (I say that with sarcasm) and jumped out of my arms to "attack" this guy who was walking by.

"Whoa! Easy there, Killer!" he laughed. Then he dug into his pocket, pulled out a doggy treat, knelt down, and held it out. "I'm your friend! See?"

Creampuff stopped barking, and after sniffing the stranger's hand, he happily accepted the treat, wagged his tail, and then licked the guy's face.

"Dude! He's nicer to you than he is to me, and I've been feeding him and picking up his poop for five years!" I exclaimed.

"Yeah, Yorkies are a little high-strung. But they're friendly once they warm up to you," he explained.

"So, you're like the Dog Whisperer. How did you learn to be so good with dogs?" I asked.

"Actually, I spend WAY too much time with them," he laughed. "I volunteer at Fuzzy Friends Animal Rescue Center."

"I'm no dog trainer, but I can give Creampuff a bath without drowning him!" I joked. "Does Fuzzy Friends need a dog washer?"

That's how Brandon and I became good friends. He's pretty cool, and we hang out at Fuzzy Friends once a week, taking care of the dogs there.

And, unlike Thug, Brandon isn't hanging around me just because he thinks my dad is Darth Vader.

What can I say? Some people drink at the fountain of knowledge, while others (like Thug) just GARGLE and SPIT!

4. SOMEBODY GET ME A DIAPER! QUICK!

Dang! I have to PEE really, really bad!

I know! You're probably thinking, DUDE! THAT'S WAY TOO MUCH INFORMATION!

But for some reason I always have to go to the bathroom whenever I get really nervous or freaked out about something.

My bladder problem has completely WRECKED my life on more than one occasion.

Like when I ALMOST came in first place in the 100-meter dash at our school's Field Day last week.

I'm not gonna lie. Getting recruited as a running back for the football team and hanging out with the popular kids would have completely changed my life.

But, unfortunately, right at the end of the race I suddenly had to take a little . . . um, DETOUR. . . .

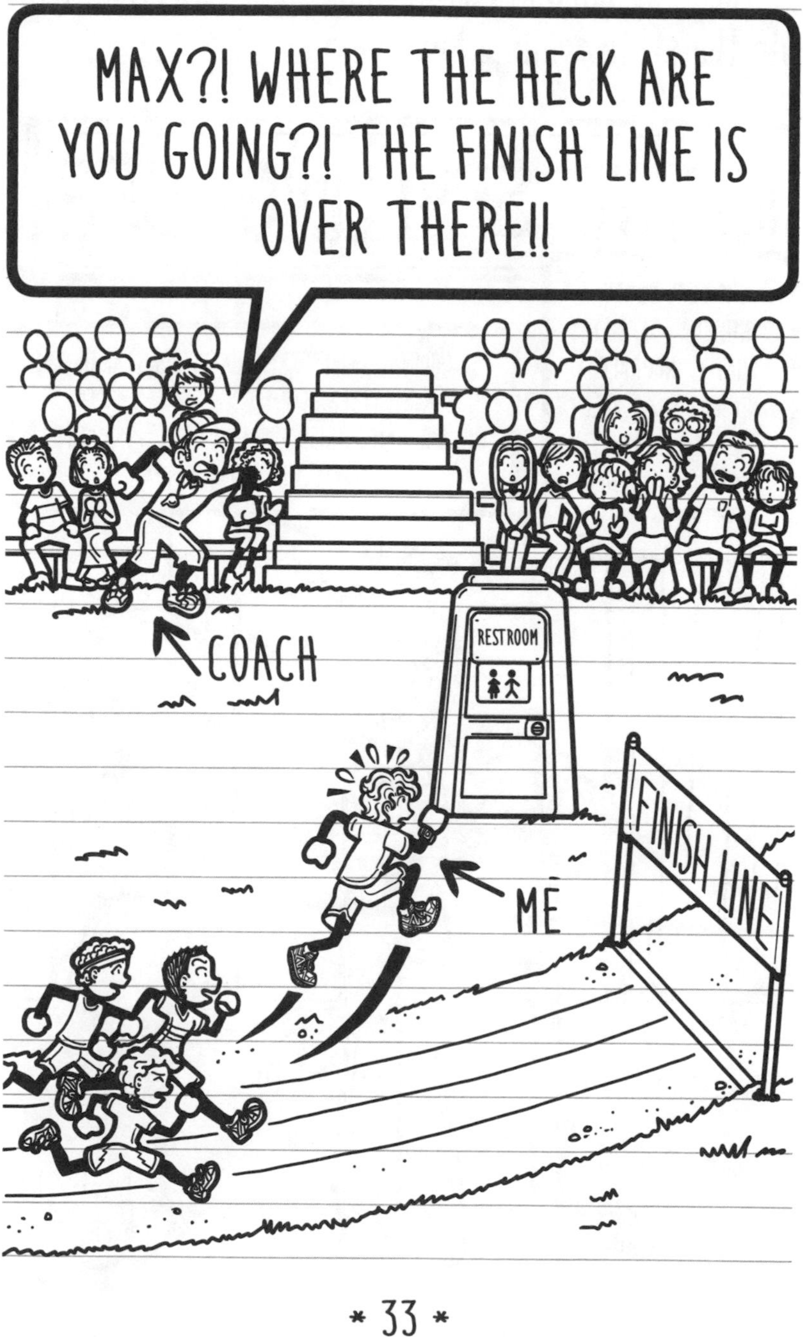
MAX?! WHERE THE HECK ARE YOU GOING?! THE FINISH LINE IS OVER THERE!!
COACH
RESTROOM
FINISH LINE
ME

Or the time back in fifth grade when I was about to win the state spelling bee championship. . . .

* 34 *

My little problem even ruined my rep with the ladies as a PARTY ANIMAL!! . . .

SORRY, ARIANA! I'D LIKE TO SIT WITH YOU AT LUNCH TO TALK ABOUT YOUR PARTY. BUT RIGHT NOW I REALLY GOTTA GO! TO . . . UM, A FUNERAL! MY POOR GRANDMA . . . UM, SNEEZED, SWALLOWED HER DENTURES, AND CHOKED TO DEATH!

OMG, MAX! THEN DON'T WORRY ABOUT MY PARTY. I'LL JUST GIVE YOUR INVITATION TO JACOB!

BOYS' RESTROOM

THE MOST POPULAR GIRL IN SCHOOL!

YEP! I got myself UNINVITED to the ONLY party I'd ever been invited to in my ENTIRE life.

Pretty PATHETIC! Right?!

But my mom is a nurse, and she tells me not to worry about my socially dysfunctional bladder.

She says my reaction is perfectly normal and just part of the automatic fight-or-flight response that both humans and animals have to protect themselves.

They sometimes dump their bladders (and even their bowels) so they can be lighter to either FIGHT their enemies or RUN away from them.

Which got me thinking about MY situation. Maybe if I had just used my natural fight-or-flight instinct, I wouldn't be STUCK inside my locker.

I mean, what if things had gone down a lot differently? You know, like THIS. . . .

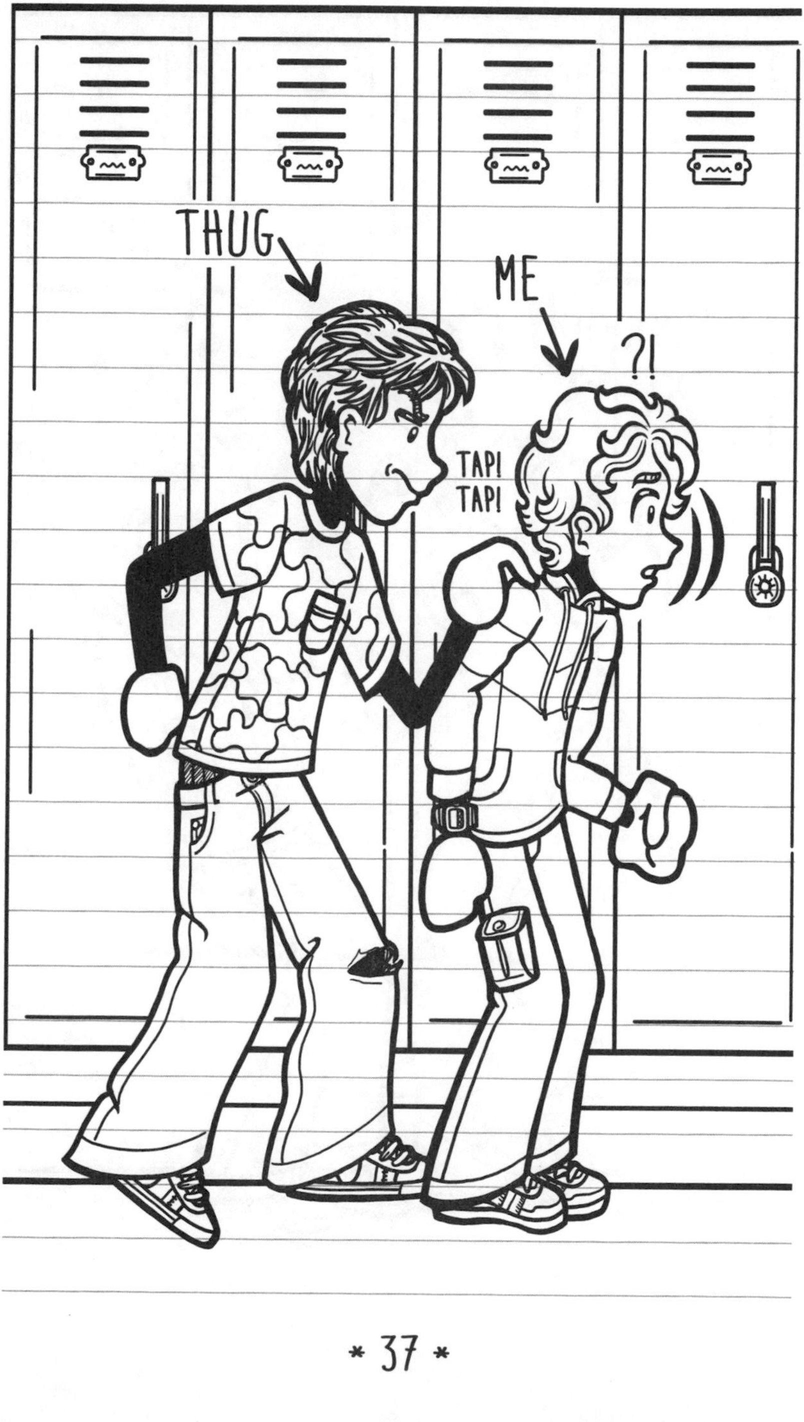
THUG
ME
?!
TAP!
TAP!

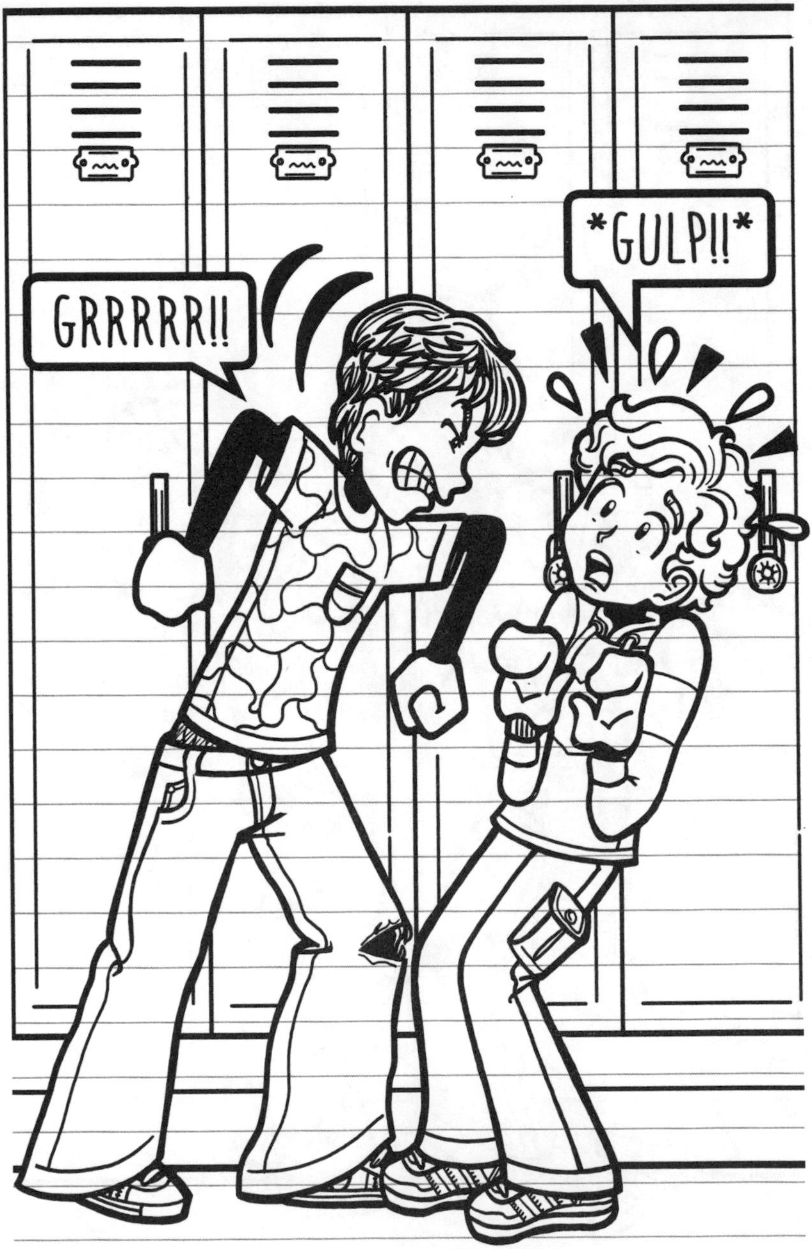
GRRRRR!!
GULP!!

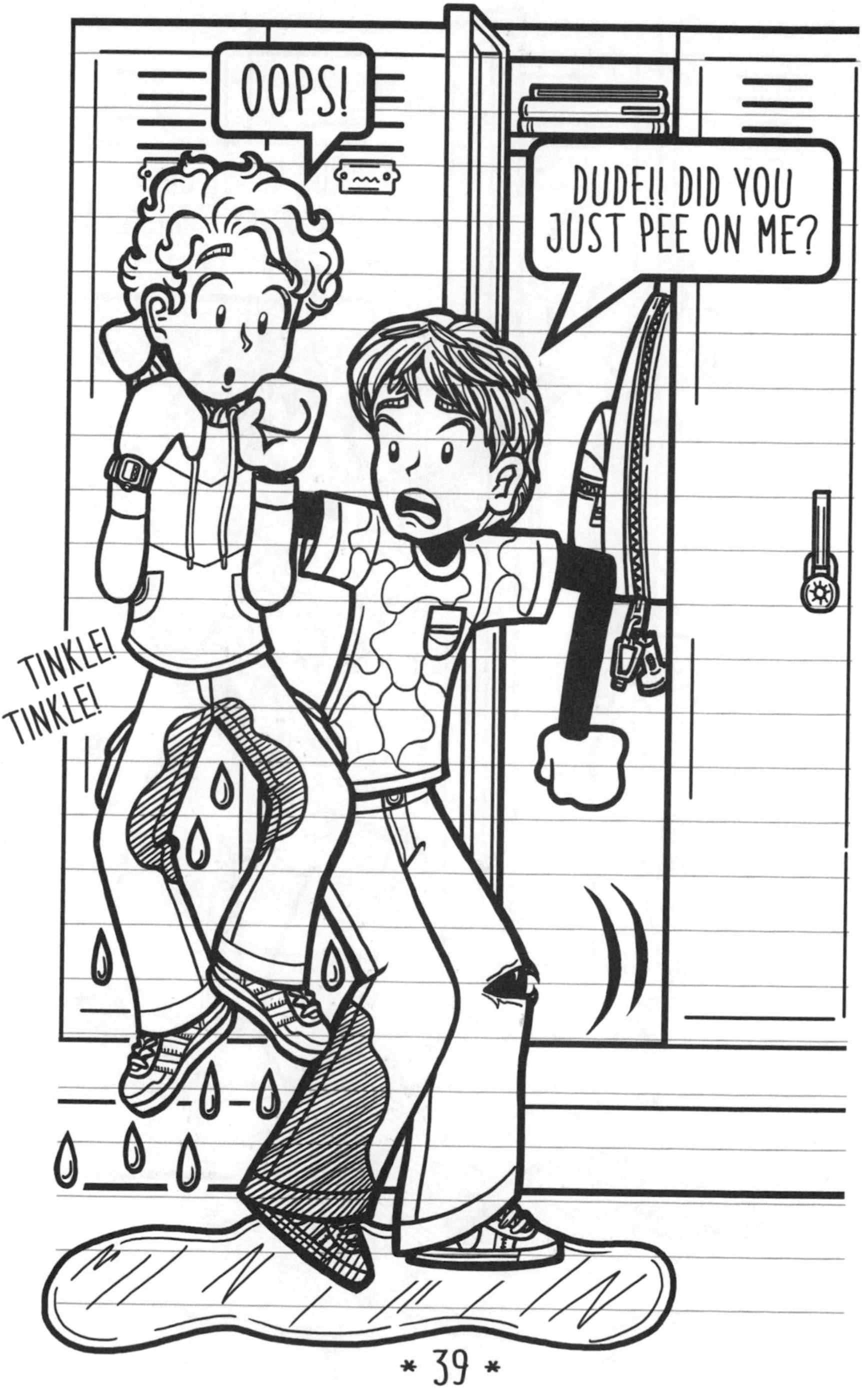
OOPS!
DUDE!! DID YOU JUST PEE ON ME?
TINKLE! TINKLE!

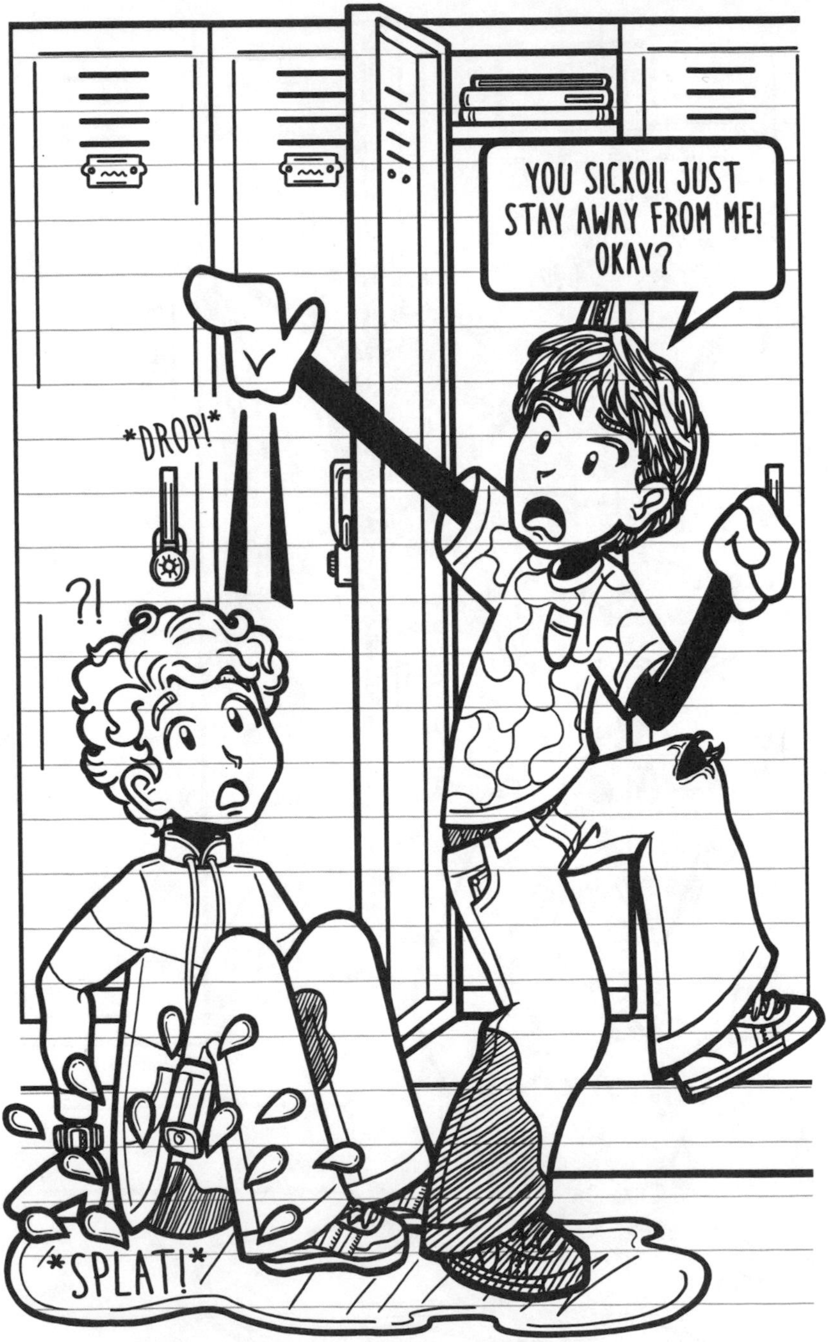
YOU SICKO!! JUST STAY AWAY FROM ME! OKAY?
DROP!
?!
SPLAT!

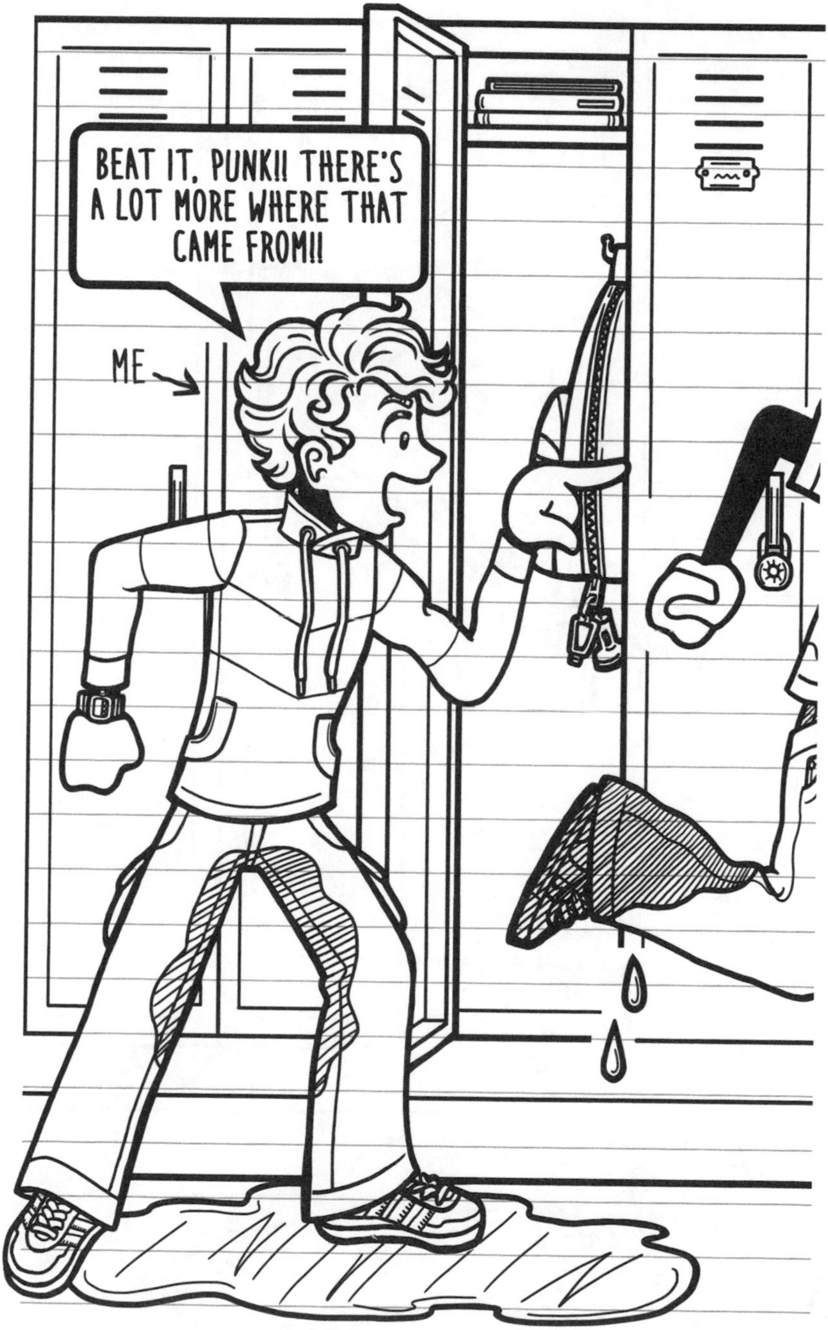
BEAT IT, PUNK!! THERE'S A LOT MORE WHERE THAT CAME FROM!!
ME

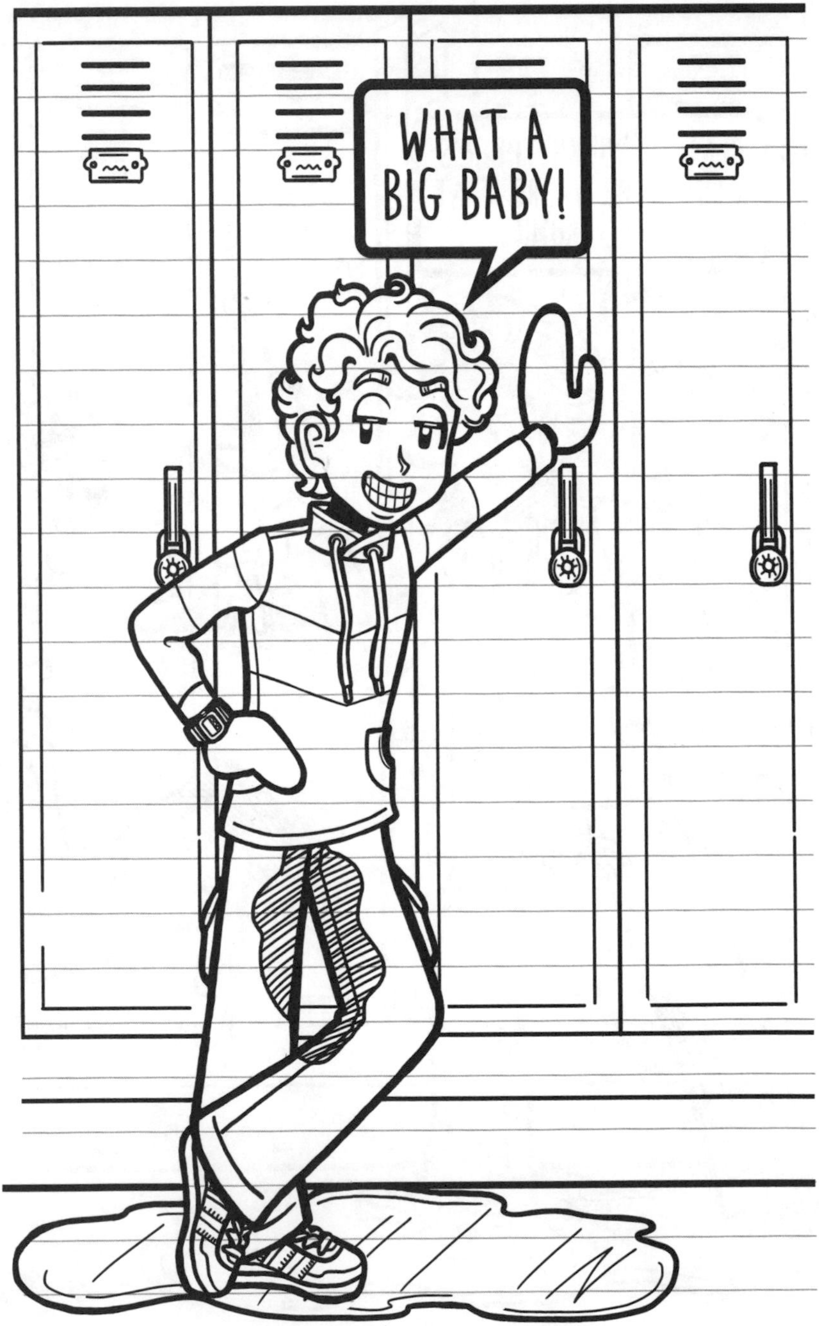
WHAT A
BIG BABY!

I bet Thug would be so freaked out and scared of me that he'd NEVER bother me again!!

And he'd even stop bullying other kids, because he'd be afraid that I'd find out about it and ~~pee on him again!~~ KICK HIS BUTT like last time!

I'd be a HERO at South Ridge Middle School, and everyone would want to be my friend and hang out with me.

How SWEET would THAT be?!!

Yeah, right. WHO am I kidding?!

I'd probably just be known at school as the WEIRD new kid who PEED on Thug Thurston!

Now THAT would really help my STREET CRED.

NOT!

5. WHY I STUCK MY TOES IN MY SISTER'S BOWL OF POPCORN

I have a huge collection of superhero comic books, and I actually write and draw my own.

I'm NOT going to LIE to you. I take all of this stuff VERY seriously.

I've done a ton of research on what it would take to become a real superhero, and it's extremely complicated and pretty intense.

Like, for example, the whole superpower thing.

Unfortunately, my uncanny, almost superhuman ability to smell pizza from a block away won't save any lives.

And the double-jointed, extra-long claw-like TOES I inherited from my father won't help me stop a criminal dead in his tracks. Although, weird toes could be invaluable in helping a wannabe-superhero-in-training scavenge for food. HOW?

I simply place my claw-like toes in my older sister Megan's bowl of popcorn and ask innocently . . .

ME, SCAVENGING FOR FOOD WITH MY SUPERHUMAN CLAW-LIKE TOES (WHILE TRAUMATIZING MY SISTER)!

This will effectively gross her out SO badly that she'll shriek, roll her eyes at me, and angrily stomp off to her bedroom to call her "BFF" and rant about how much she HATES MY GUTS!

Basically leaving said bowl of hot, buttery popcorn unattended for MY eating pleasure. YUM!!

The other major headache is putting together a cool superhero costume that makes evil villains tremble in their boots at the mere sight of you. . . .

✹✹ SUPERHERO COSTUME DON'TS ✹✹

1. DON'T buy one of those cheap kiddie costumes that you can get on clearance at your local dollar store the week AFTER Halloween.

No one will take you seriously as Super Ghost if you're wearing a white plastic tablecloth with big green eyeballs on it and a red sticker on your chest that says CLEARANCE! ALL SALES FINAL!

2. DON'T let your MOM make you a "supercute"

homemade costume. Especially if it includes glitter, feathers, fake diamonds, more glitter, sequins, the color pink, even more glitter, and/or platform boots.

Also, absolutely REFUSE to let her talk you into calling yourself Super Glittery Guy because the costume she made you is "totally FIERCE"!

3. DON'T recycle one of your tacky OLD Halloween costumes. EVER! Always remember! Recycling is for cans and plastic bottles. NOT superhero costumes.

Unfortunately, I learned Rule #3 the hard way.

My grandma spent two months sewing me an authentic costume of an iconic hero that was adored by her and millions of fans around the world back in 1964. He was known for performing superhuman moves never before seen by mankind.

I STILL have very traumatic recurring nightmares about that costume. . . .

ME, IN MY RECYCLED ELVIS SUPERHERO
COSTUME, POWER ROCKING WITH MY
MIGHTY MICROPHONE OF DOOM!!

WARNING!! Never forget that superheroes are SUPER sensitive about their costumes.

Do you have any idea how many people have actually DIED after DISSING a superhero's costume?!

Approximately seven citizens and nineteen villains.

Electrostatic Man actually ZAPPED his OWN MOTHER with 10,000 watts after she accidentally called his ultra-thin nylon protective leg gear . . .

PANTYHOSE!!

Of course, everyone in the superhero world was shocked, appalled, and outraged when they heard what had happened.

That heinous act was cruel and disrespectful on so many levels.

The good news is that Electrostatic Man's MOTHER won't EVER make THAT stupid mistake again!

6. YES, BAT KID IS MY LITTLE BROTHER!

Okay, I love my grandma as much as the next kid.

But I'm really desperate to make this public school thing work! HOW desperate am I?

So desperate that I sold part of my priceless comic book collection and bought some new clothes for the first day of school.

I'd heard over and over again that in middle school, IMAGE is everything!

So I decided I was going to be the most WICKED, FRESH, FLY, DOPE (and all those other slang words that won't even be cool anymore by the time you read this) dude at my school!

Don't get me wrong! It WASN'T a makeover. It was more like a virtual software update to make me BETTER!

Meet MAXWELL CRUMBLY 2.0! The REMIX!! . . .

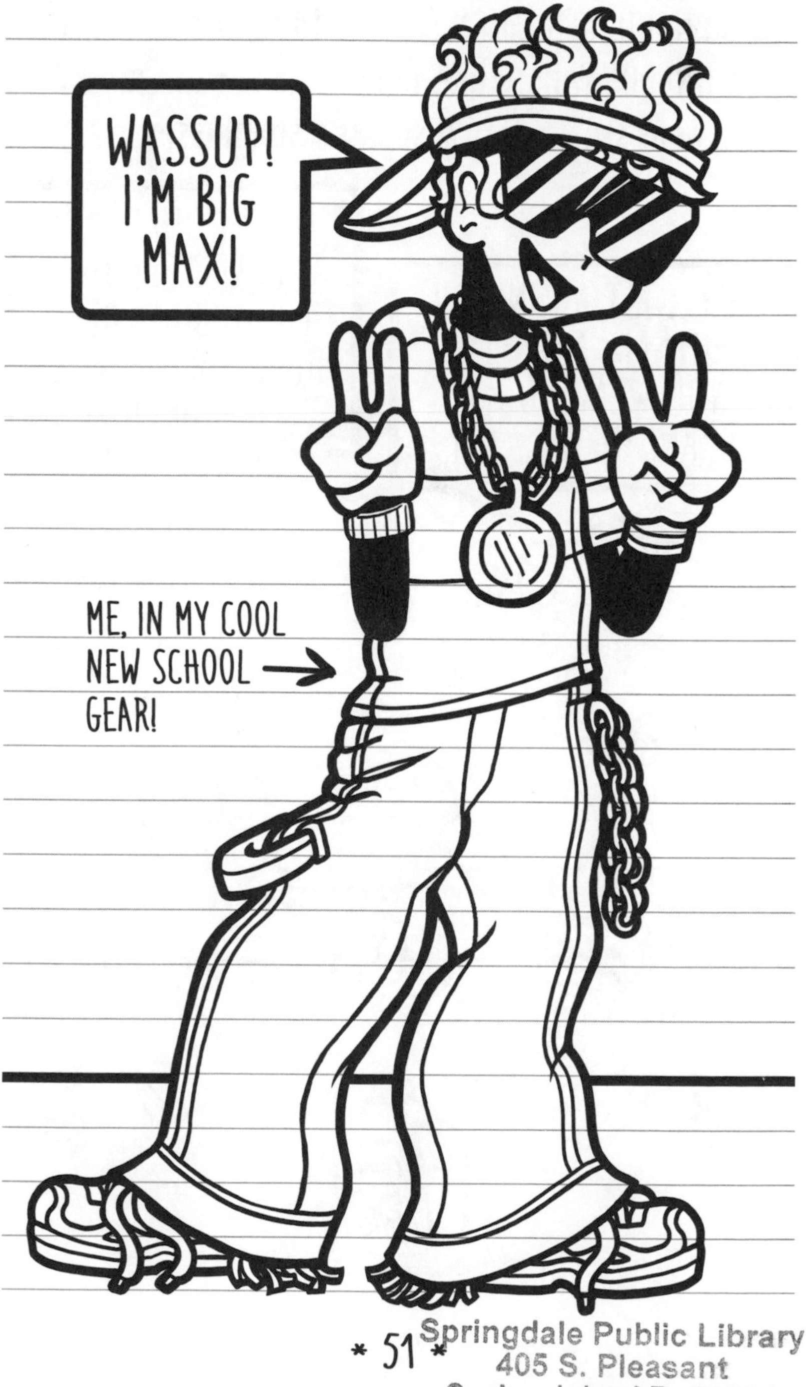
WASSUP! I'M BIG MAX!
ME, IN MY COOL NEW SCHOOL GEAR!

You have NO IDEA how hard it is to be a trendsetter in an UNCOOL family like mine. First of all, my EVIL sister kept swiping my visor and sunglasses. . . .

Then my MOM borrowed my gold chain to wear to her best friend's birthday party. . . .

Then there was that little problem with my dad. . . .

Okay, I KNOW my new pants were five sizes too BIG.

But they're SUPPOSED to be baggy!

I was like, "Dad, you're kidding me! Right?!"

A father and son sharing pants?!

Sorry! But that's just . . . WRONG on so many levels!

The final straw was my little brother, Oliver.

I saved up my own money for an entire year and finally managed to buy a pair of AIR JORDAN sneakers!

I ~~totally lost it~~ got really annoyed when the little brat trashed them with a permanent black marker!!!

Apparently, Oliver is just starting to learn his ABCs. But he obviously DOESN'T quite have the hang of it yet. . . .

MY MESSED-UP JAYS

Is it just me, or are all those frowny faces Oliver drew on my shoes possibly a sign of some underlying emotional problem that will manifest itself during his teen years?

I think our pastor is a little worried about him too. Like me, Oliver is into superheroes. But he's taken it A LOT further than I EVER did! . . .

?!

"SO, DO WE HAVE ANY VISITORS TODAY?
UM . . . OKAY, I SEE WE HAVE ONE . . . !"

Of course, all the kids (and a few of the dads) were really excited to see what they thought was a real, live superhero sitting in the front row.

So when the service was over, there was actually a line of fans wanting to take selfies with Oliver.

Sorry, but it's NOT easy being BAT KID's brother!

Anyway, by the time the first day of school rolled around, I just wasn't feeling those new clothes anymore.

But can you blame me? My family had taken all the COOLNESS out of my back-to-school style. And completely KILLED IT!

I was so FRUSTRATED with the whole situation that I just DUMPED them in one of those clothing bins at the local Goodwill.

THEM meaning my clothes!

NOT my FAMILY! . . .

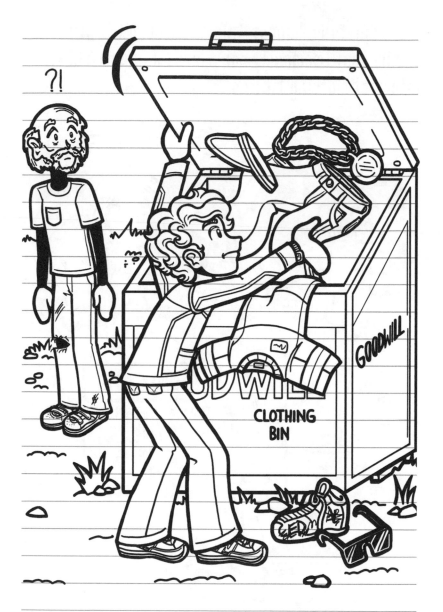

ME, DONATING MY CLOTHES
TO THE LESS FORTUNATE

Although, to be honest, I was so TICKED OFF at my family that I seriously considered dumping THEM into that clothing bin too....

ME, DONATING MY FAMILY TO WHOEVER WILL TAKE THEM!

Maybe one day I'll try wearing some hip-hop gear again.

But it's definitely going to be AFTER I put a dead bolt lock on my bedroom door.

Hey, I love my family as much as the next guy.

And by "love," I mean that 49% of the time I DON'T want to punch them in the face.

But don't get it twisted!

I'm just NOT into sharing my pants and stuff with them.

Sorry, that's just too . . . **WEIRD!!**

7. SIPPIN' PRUNE JUICE
FROM A RED PLASTIC CUP

I had pretty much forgotten that I'd donated my new school clothes to charity. But about a week later my mom made me take Oliver to the local park to play.

And while he was having fun, I decided to find a park bench and finish reading my latest comic book.

I totally FREAKED when I saw this old guy chilling out with a cup of prune juice. Because guess what he was wearing?

MY brand-new school clothes!!

That dude looked like an eighty-three-year-old Eminem.

I think the pigeons were a little freaked out too, because a half dozen of them had gathered around and were just staring at the guy like he was a giant piece of birdseed or something. . . .

ME AND THE PIGEONS ARE FREAKED OUT TO SEE AN OLD DUDE WEARING MY NEW SCHOOL CLOTHES!

Although all of this was a little traumatic for me, it was also kind of inspiring. It felt good that someone seemed happy to be wearing my school clothes. Well, someone other than my OWN family members!

When I got home, I wrote a very cool rap about what it would be like if I were an elderly old-school rapper. It's actually the BEST material I've ever written. . . .

* *

SIPPIN' PRUNE JUICE FROM A RED PLASTIC CUP (THE SUPER-COOL RAPPER OLD MAX C.)

Mic check! Mic check!
Yo! 1-2-3!
The best rapper in the world
is Old Max C.!

Spittin' rhymes and rockin',
just tryin' to get paid!
Say what? Say what?
I need a hearing aid!

When I crash a party,
people stop and stare.
'Cause I'm chillin' like a villain,
Rollin' in my wheelchair.

I got a diamond grill!
What's up! What's up!
And some gold false teeth
both soaking in a cup.

If you wanna hear the truth,
don't listen to a liar.
I'm NOT the Real Slim Shady,
but I'm spittin' FIRE!

All the haters be hatin'
'cause my rhymes don't stop.
And today I wanna say . . . !
Oops! I forgot!

Now wave your canes
in the air!
We're wearing diapers, and we
just don't care!

Get your bingo on
till the break of dawn.
If you're MEAN, then SCREAM,
"HEY! GET OFF MY LAWN!!"

Besides my mind,
I got nothing to lose.
Stylin' in my blinged-out
Velcro shoes!

If you're feelin' this rap,
stand up and dance!
I boogied so hard
that I POOPED my pants!

I'm sippin' prune juice
from a red plastic cup,
screaming, "Help me! I've fallen,
and I can't get up!"

Mic check! Mic check!
Yo! 1-2-3!
Don't you wanna be a rapper
like Old Max C.?

* *

Hey, I don't want to brag, but this rap is DOPE!

Personally, I think I could have a really long and successful rap career that might last well into my eighties.

And I'd make a boatload of CASH too!!

FOR REAL!!

8. JUST CALL ME BARF!

I don't have the slightest idea why Thug Thurston HATES me so much.

I NEVER did anything to him.

On purpose, anyway.

But I guess there WAS that little accident in PE class.

The one that earned me the nickname BARF.

Hey, don't laugh. It was actually pretty scary at the time.

We were in PE doing the rope climb. You have to climb up a thirty-foot rope to the gym ceiling, ring a bell, and then slide down. All in only sixty seconds.

I was feeling really nervous because I HATE heights. . . .

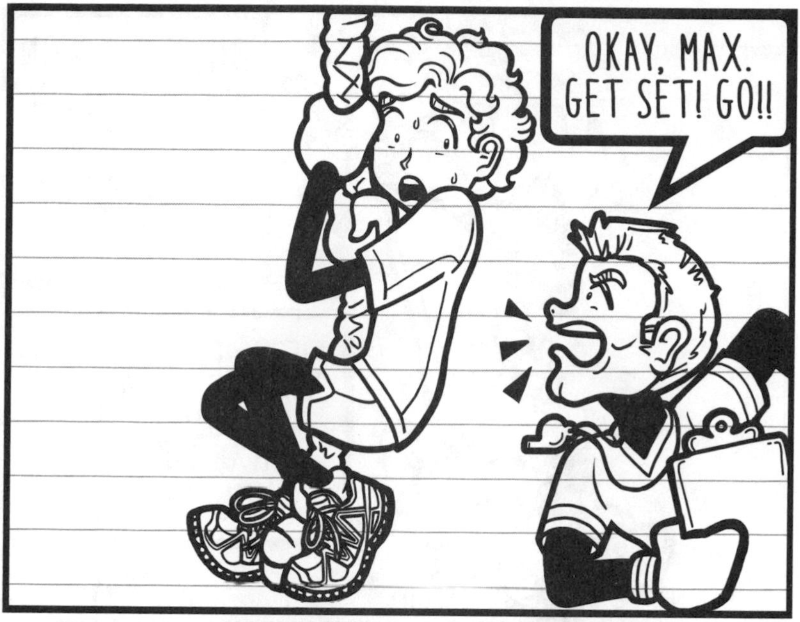
OKAY, MAX.
GET SET! GO!!

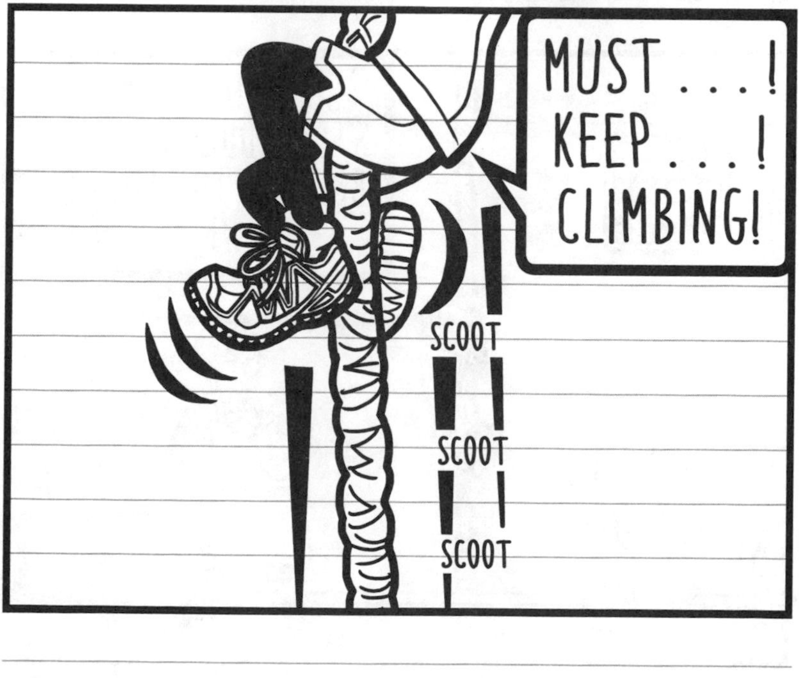
MUST . . . !
KEEP . . . !
CLIMBING!
SCOOT
SCOOT
SCOOT

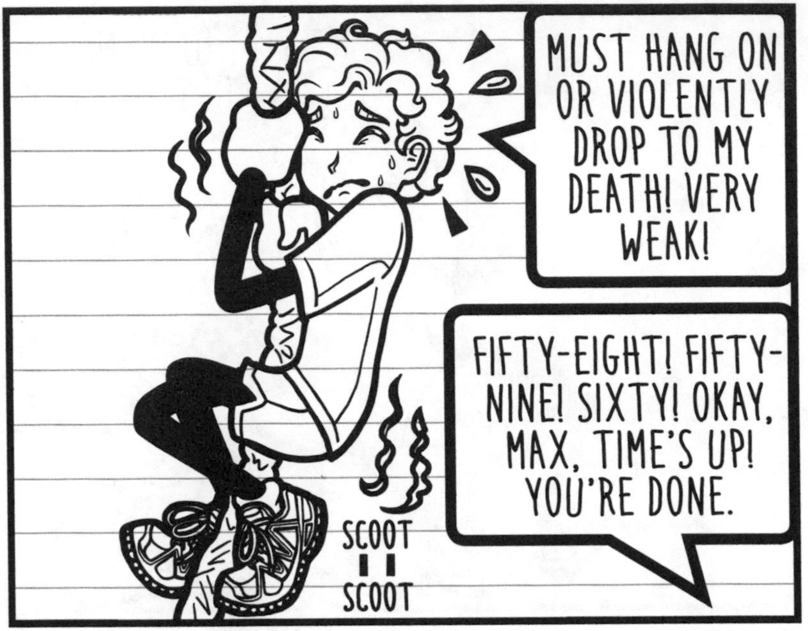
MUST HANG ON OR VIOLENTLY DROP TO MY DEATH! VERY WEAK!
FIFTY-EIGHT! FIFTY-NINE! SIXTY! OKAY, MAX, TIME'S UP! YOU'RE DONE.
SCOOT SCOOT

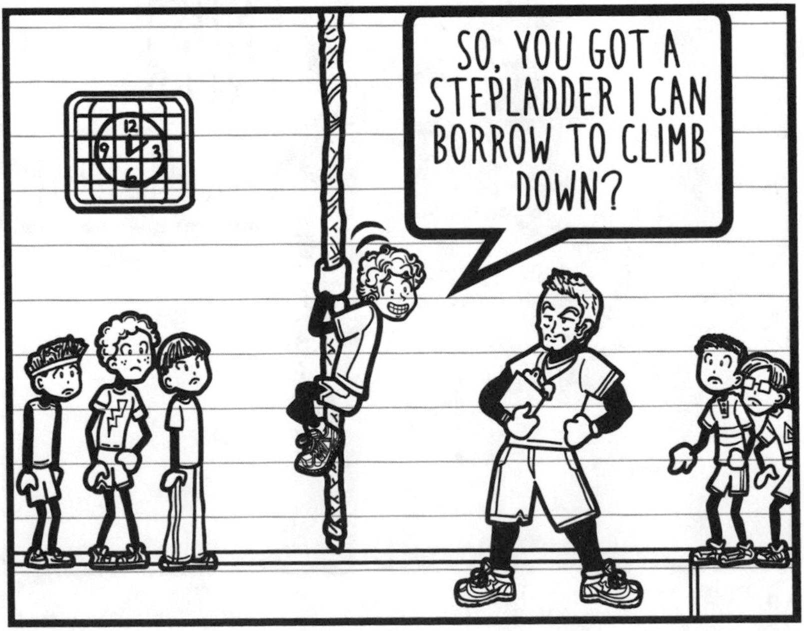
SO, YOU GOT A STEPLADDER I CAN BORROW TO CLIMB DOWN?

I couldn't believe I had only climbed up that stupid rope a measly twenty-nine inches. It felt like a mile.

I guess I didn't need that stepladder after all.

But afterward I felt so dizzy and queasy, I actually THREW UP my oatmeal! Right there in the gym. . . .

ON THUG THURSTON'S FOOT!!!

The whole thing was surreal.

That guy was SO mad, I could almost see steam coming out of his ears like a cartoon character or something.

Our teacher shook his head in disgust and went to get a janitor to clean up the mess I'd made.

That's when Thug got right up in my face, so close I could smell the STANK from the baloney, mustard, and egg sandwich he had eaten for breakfast.

I swear!! It smelled so bad I almost puked AGAIN!

On his OTHER foot!! For REAL!!

Then he snarled, "Yo! PUNK! I should rip your head right off your shoulders, dribble it across the floor, and . . ."

He shot an imaginary basket.

"SWISH!! What do you think of that, BARF?!"

I did NOT appreciate that guy dissing me in front of the entire PE class and calling me out like that.

Hey, dude! My name is Max Crumbly!

However, for health reasons, I decided it would probably be a good idea for me to ALSO answer to the name BARF.

"What do I think of YOU ripping my head off and shooting a basket with it? Actually, um . . . I'm a little attached to my head. So why don't you just rip off something else?" I answered nervously. . . .

THUG, RIPPING OFF MY HEAD AND
SHOOTING A BASKET WITH IT!!

Everyone in the class started snickering at my accidentally sarcastic answer.

Which, of course, made Thug even MORE angry at me.

This is what I wanted to say to him. . . .

"Dude! Just chill out! That vomit on your shoe is the LEAST of your problems. Have you looked in the mirror lately? Your acne is so BAD it looks like your face caught on fire and someone tried to put it out with a fork!!"

But because I'm a peaceful person and very allergic to beatdowns, I thought I should at least apologize for my accident to squash our beef.

"Um . . . s-sorry, bro! For r-real!" I stammered.

"You don't look that sorry to ME!" Thug fumed.

Then he grabbed me by the collar of my T-shirt and actually growled at me like an angry pit bull or something. . . .

THUG, REALLY TICKED OFF THAT
I THREW UP ON HIS SHOE!

Thank goodness the PE teacher came back, and just in time, too. He stared at us like he knew something was about to go down.

Thug whispered some not-so-nice words under his breath and pushed me away.

"THURSTON! Go clean off your shoe! And why are the rest of y'all standing around here like a parade is coming or something? Give me three laps around the gym! Move it!" the teacher yelled like an army drill sergeant. "Come on, people! Get the lead out! Hustle!"

Okay! This is what I wanted to know. If I was already blowin' chunks of oatmeal, WHY would the teacher make ME run three laps around the gym?!

WHAT an IDIOT!!

But I wasn't about to stand there and argue with the guy. So I just sucked it up and started running laps too.

The oatmeal vomit fiasco is probably why Thug HATES me to this day. And now, every chance he gets, he hunts me down like an animal and makes my life MISERABLE.

I know! I know! You're probably thinking, Why not just report Thug to the principal and be done with it? He'd get detention or maybe even be expelled.

To be honest, I've thought about doing that a million times. I'm just worried that the principal might tell my parents and they'd pull me out of this school.

But here's the word on the street! . . .

I heard at lunch yesterday that Thug's parents are getting a divorce. And there's a chance he'll be moving to another city at the end of the school year.

Very BAD news for HIM! **BOO-HOO!** But very GOOD news for ME! **WOO-HOO!**

I was SO relieved that Thug might possibly move that I actually did my VICTORY DANCE!...

Thug might be mov-ing!

Thug might be mov-ing!

So, the way I see it, I basically have to survive EITHER . . .

ONE year at South Ridge Middle School with Thug!

Or FIVE ~~very long, agonizing~~ years of homeschooling with my grandma!

Hey! Call me a zit-faced glutton for punishment, but at this point, I choose . . .

THUG!

Sorry 'bout that, Grandma.

9. HOW I ACCIDENTALLY BUSTED MY PANTS, BASHED MY KNEE, AND BRUISED MY EGO

Okay, if this scene were in one of my favorite comic books, it would be written like this. . . .

"When we last left our hero, he was trapped inside the deep, dark bowels of his locker, imprisoned there, for perhaps eternity, by his evil archnemesis, Thug Thurston. However, using his stealth and cunning, our hero communicates telepathically with a nearby alien life-form in an attempt to summon help!"

So maybe desperately banging on my locker door while screaming hysterically like a scared toddler WASN'T exactly telepathic or very heroic. But still! It worked.

Through the small vents in the door, I saw a startled girl freeze in her tracks. Then she slowly approached my locker and stared at it with a perplexed look on her face. . . .

THE FABULOUS VIEW FROM
INSIDE MY LOCKER!!

* 81 *

Thank goodness! Help at last! But when I finally recognized just WHO she was, my heart dropped into my socks.

It was Erin Madison! THE ~~cutest and~~ smartest girl in the entire eighth grade. She was also president of the computer club ~~which was one of the main reasons I wanted to join it.~~

We'd had a really deep conversation in science class the first week of school.

I was handing in my extra-credit homework about the largest carnivorous (meat-eating) dinosaurs when she'd smiled at me and said, "Wow! Did you draw those dinos? You're a super-talented artist!"

After I checked to make sure she wasn't talking to someone behind me, I gave her a goofy grin, shrugged, and then just kind of stared at her.

I was really nervous. Somehow I tripped over the trash can, fell over, split my pants, banged my knee on the floor, and screamed, "OW! DANG, THAT HURT!"

Of course, Thug and most of the kids in my class laughed and told me what a total KLUTZ I was.

I was SO embarrassed and humiliated! ~~I wanted to shove the trash can over my head, crawl out of the room to the nearest bathroom, and FLUSH myself down the toilet.~~

"OMG! Are you okay?" Erin had exclaimed as she helped me up.

But I just nodded, covered the gaping hole in the back of my pants ~~(that was exposing my official, vintage Superman logo underwear that I'd purchased on eBay, thinking that one day they'd be worth a boatload of money)~~ with my science book, and limped away as quickly as I could on a totally busted kneecap.

Yes! I'd made a complete FOOL of myself!

So I was surprised when Erin actually stopped to talk to me a few days later. Everything was perfect! For about fifteen seconds. . . .

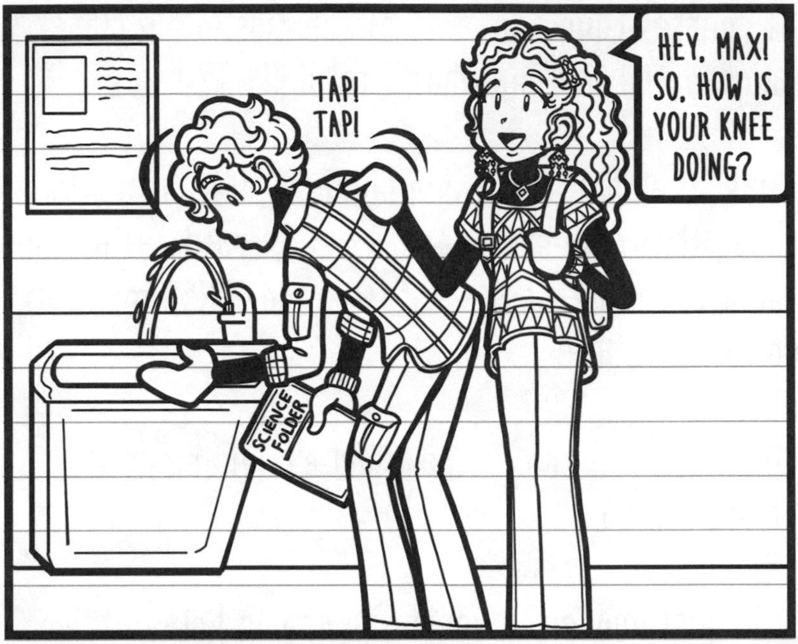
HEY, MAX! SO, HOW IS YOUR KNEE DOING?
TAP! TAP!
SCIENCE FOLDER

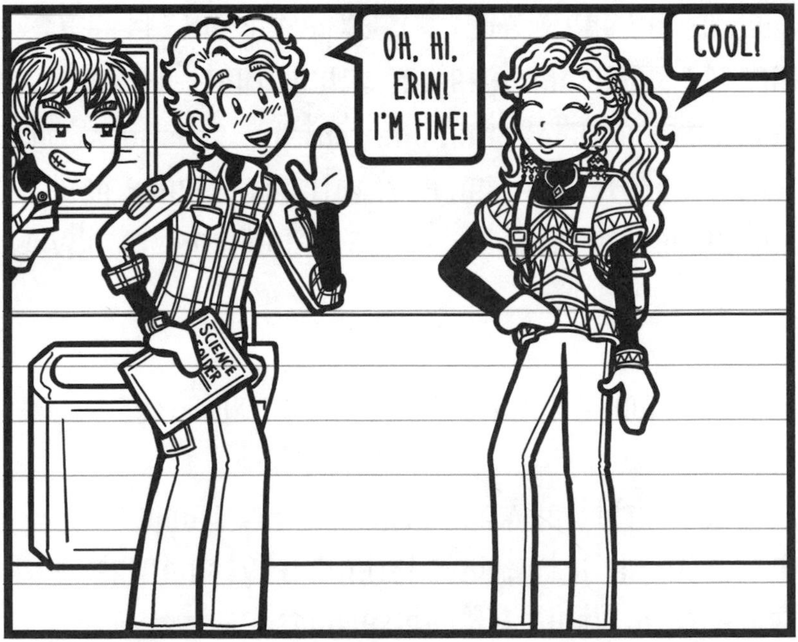
OH, HI, ERIN! I'M FINE!
COOL!

I couldn't believe Thug just came out of nowhere and bumped into me like that.

I dropped my science folder, and papers went flying everywhere!

Erin was about to go off on Thug, until he apologized and pretended the whole thing was a big accident.

And get this! He actually told her that he loved her shirt and that magenta was his favorite color.

YEAH, RIGHT!
That dude couldn't even SPELL magenta!

Watching Thug trying to flirt with Erin like that was really annoying. I was happy when he finally decided to get lost.

Anyway, Erin offered to help pick up my papers that were scattered all over the floor. But it made me SUPER nervous. . . .

I started grabbing papers as fast as I could and stuffing them back into my folder before Erin saw any of my drawings.

Because NO JOKE! I was literally going to DIE OF EMBARRASSMENT if she saw a secret sketch that I'd drawn earlier that week during lunch.

What was it?

None of your ding-dang BUSINESS!!

Okay, FINE! I'll tell you! I'd drawn a sketch of . . . ERIN!!

And of course I didn't want her to ~~know~~ think I was some SICKO who snuck around secretly drawing people behind their backs.

I broke into a cold sweat and almost had a panic attack when Erin picked up the very LAST piece of paper!

And it was (you guessed it!) . . .

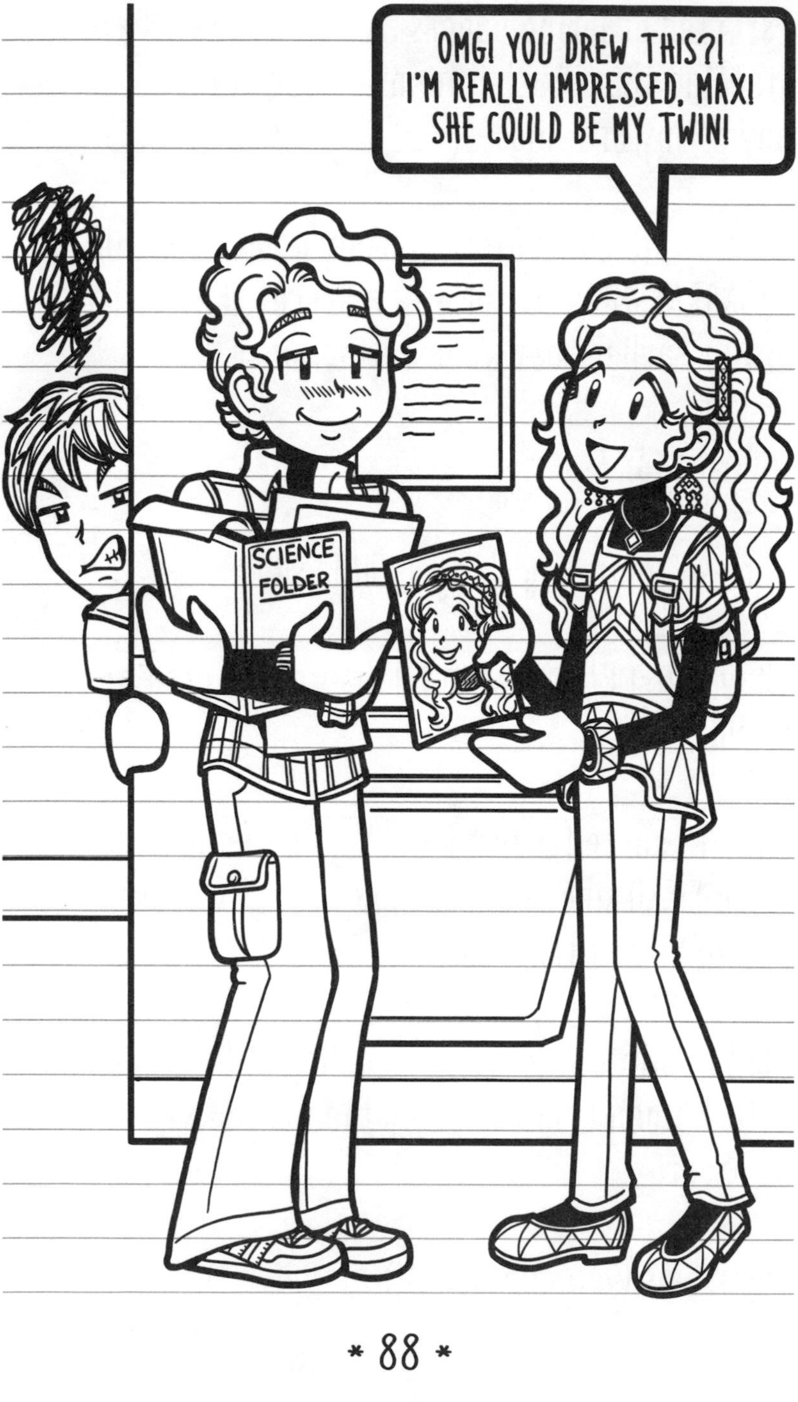
OMG! YOU DREW THIS?! I'M REALLY IMPRESSED, MAX! SHE COULD BE MY TWIN!
SCIENCE FOLDER

As Erin stared at the drawing again, I quickly ~~snatched it~~ grabbed it from her and shoved it back into my folder.

"Wow, you're right! She COULD be your twin! What a strange coincidence." I shrugged and quickly changed the subject. "Thanks for the compliment. I really like drawing, and it's kind of my hobby."

"Hey, you should enter our avant-garde art competition! It's next month, I think. Every middle school has one."

Actually, Brandon had suggested the same thing to me too.

He said I had awesome skillz and was "almost" as good an artist as his friend Nikki Maxwell, who is entering the avant-garde art competition at his school.

But I think he's probably crushing on that girl, because he talks about her ALL the time.

So, if you ask me, he's TOTALLY biased about who's the better artist. I'm just saying!

"Listen, Max, I know this is kind of last minute, but would you be interested in painting some background scenes for the school play? We're doing *The Ice Princess*, and I'm part of the cast. But I'm also the director and stage manager. And unless additional people show up to help, I'll probably end up having to do even more. I might be the audience, too!" she joked.

"It sounds like you have your hands full!" I said.

"Totally! My mom and I just finished making my costume yesterday. And if things don't improve, our advisor says we might have to cancel the play this year!" Erin said, sounding a bit frustrated.

"Cancel it?! That would be awful! I've never painted scenes before, but it sounds like fun," I said.

"Great! I could definitely use your help. Can you meet after school today in the theater classroom? I'll bring all the paint and supplies."

"Cool! I'm really looking forward to it." I smiled.

"Okay! Bye, Max. And thanks a million for agreeing to help out!"

"No problem! Thanks for asking me. Bye, Erin," I said as I watched her disappear down the hall.

I couldn't believe that I'd finally made my very first friend at South Ridge Middle School.

And it was Erin Madison!!

How COOL was THAT?!

With a big goofy smile plastered across my face, I turned around to head off to class, and . . .

BAM!

THUG slammed into me! AGAIN!

Only it was like hitting a brick wall. A very STUPID brick wall!

Why did it feel like running into that guy was suddenly becoming a really BAD habit?!

"Stay out of my way, BARF!" he spat. "Are you trying to start something? Because if you are, I'll be happy to give you a BEATDOWN after school today. Right after I finish detention."

"Actually, Thug-er, I mean Doug-you kind of bumped into ME," I explained.

"Wait a minute! Are you blaming ME?!" Thug snarled.

"No, I just was trying to explain how-"

"SHUT UP, BARF! You can explain it after school. To my FIST!!"

Then he shoved me and walked away.

I didn't have the slightest idea where all of that CRAZY had suddenly come from.

But it was definitely weird how Thug had been hanging around the ENTIRE time I was talking to Erin. Suddenly it hit me! Maybe Thug LIKED Erin ~~too~~!!

THUG IN LOVE!

One thing was for certain! Thug or no Thug, I had no intention of bailing on Erin after I had promised to help her.

Especially after she told me the play was already in jeopardy of being canceled.

10. GRANDMA CHOKES ON HER DENTURES AND DIES! (AGAIN.)

Okay, I LIED!

I had no intention whatsoever of BAILING on Erin, UNTIL later that afternoon I heard some football players talking about "the big fight after school today."

And it was going to be between THUG and some new kid named MAX CRUMMY?!

Just GREAT!!

Some days you're the BUG, and some days you're the windshield!

And, unfortunately, that day I was the BUG!

As much as I wanted to help Erin, I knew I had to avoid trouble with Thug or risk my parents pulling me out of South Ridge Middle School.

So I didn't have a choice but to tell Erin ~~the truth~~ some very BAD NEWS!

You know, THAT news. . . .

How I couldn't stay after school to help with the play because my grandmother had sneezed, accidentally swallowed her dentures, and choked to death!!

And I had to rush straight home to go to her FUNERAL!

But when I got to the theater room, I couldn't help but notice through the window that Erin seemed kind of down.

And she kept glancing anxiously at her watch.

Sure, I was a few minutes late.

But give me a break!

~~It wasn't like I was helping Michelangelo paint the SISTINE CHAPEL!~~

ERIN, WAITING FOR ME TO SHOW UP?

The last thing Erin needed was ~~me bailing on~~ ~~her because I was too big a COWARD to stand up~~ ~~to Thug, and then LYING about it~~ more DRAMA in her life!

With a FRIEND like me, who needs an ENEMY, right?!

So instead of giving her a lame excuse about my grandma choking on her dentures, I decided to just head for home before Thug caught up with me.

And if I hurried, I could still catch my bus.

I know! You're probably thinking, "Dude, I don't like you very much right now. And I didn't like you that much to begin with!"

I totally agree with you. Because right then I didn't like myself much either.

But in the end I COULDN'T walk away and just leave Erin hanging like that when she was depending on me.

~~And yes. I ALSO knew that I probably wouldn't be able to walk away LATER once Thug caught up with me and broke both of my legs!~~

I knocked on the window, smiled, and waved at Erin.

Hopefully, if Thug looked for me in the theater room, once he spotted Erin he'd totally forget about the fight and try to impress her by BRAGGING about more of his favorite obscure yet fashionable colors.

Erin gave me a weak smile as she opened the door.

"Thanks for coming, Max! But, actually, I don't need your help anymore. So you can go," she said as she sniffed and wiped her eyes.

"I'm really sorry I'm late! Um, are you okay, Erin?"

"Yeah, I'm fine, I guess! I just got some bad news."

"Really? What happened?" I asked, concerned.

"Well, I don't want to talk about it right now, okay? But thanks for coming. I'll see you around."

"Sure, Erin. If there's anything I can do . . ."

"No, there ISN'T. Just please leave me alone!"

BURN!!

"Um, okay." I shrugged. Then I turned and walked out of the room.

So that was it! My friendship with Erin Madison lasted barely half a day.

At that moment I was sure of only two things.

I DIDN'T understand GIRLS! AT ALL!!

And I had exactly forty-eight seconds to get my BUTT on the bus if I wanted to make it home in one piece!

11. WARNING!! BEWARE OF THE FREAKY LOCKER VAMPIRE!

So for the rest of the week, I avoided Erin like my least-favorite contagious fatal disease.

But don't get it twisted!

~~It wasn't like I was STILL crushing on her or anything like that.~~

It wasn't like I was EVER interested in her or anything like that. Hey, I barely even KNOW the GIRL!!

Although I DID catch her staring at me a couple of times in class ~~because I was sort of staring at HER.~~

But it was probably just my imagination.

Anyway, NOW you know why I was so traumatized when I realized it was Erin, of all people, outside my locker.

Unfortunately, I was about to humiliate myself AGAIN!!

ME, ACCIDENTALLY FREAKING OUT ERIN!

As she cautiously stood outside my locker, I slumped against the back wall, closed my eyes, and held my breath.

I could always just pretend like I WASN'T in here and HADN'T been screaming for help like a maniac just a few seconds ago.

Then maybe Erin would think it was just her imagination and go away.

"Hello?! Is anyone inside there?" she asked nervously.

Awkward silence.

Erin looked over her shoulder, suspecting that maybe the whole thing was a big joke being filmed for the school's website or something.

"Um . . . did someone in there just ask for help?"

More awkward silence. Erin folded her arms and bit her lip.

I could almost hear the wheels spinning in her brain as she tried to figure out what was going on.

She glanced over her shoulder to make sure no one was watching and then slowly raised her fist.

KNOCK-KNOCK!

I couldn't BELIEVE Erin had actually knocked on my locker door like that!

Unfortunately, I blurted out the first thing that popped into my head and then immediately wished I hadn't.

"Um . . . WHO'S THERE?!"

Erin seemed really surprised that I'd answered.

Heck, even I was really surprised I'd answered.

"It's me, Erin! I was just walking by and— Wait a minute! Is this some kind of joke?" she asked, highly annoyed.

"No."

"Listen, I'm in a hurry, so I don't have time to stand here talking to some weirdo in a locker. If that's your thing, fine! But I just want to make sure you're okay since you were screaming for help a minute ago."

I sighed and cleared my throat. "Um . . . yeah. I'm fine, I guess. I just seriously need to get out of here!"

"Okay, I'll get help! The principal or a teacher or maybe a janitor. Somebody! Just wait right here until I get back, okay?"

"Like, WHERE am I going to go? I'm STUCK in here. Remember?"

"Sorry! I'm just trying to help. . . ."

"Maybe I can give you my combination. As long as you can get that stupid door open, I'm good!" I muttered.

"I can try. But I have trouble getting my OWN locker open," Erin said as she spun the dial a few times. "Okay! What is it?"

"38, 12, 7," I answered.

She stared at the lock, deep in concentration.

"38, 12, 7," she repeated.

Then . . .

CLICK!

I held my breath as Erin slowly opened the locker door!

The bright hall lights flooded in, temporarily blinding me.

I blinked and squinted my eyes.

But Erin blinked and widened hers in surprise. . . .

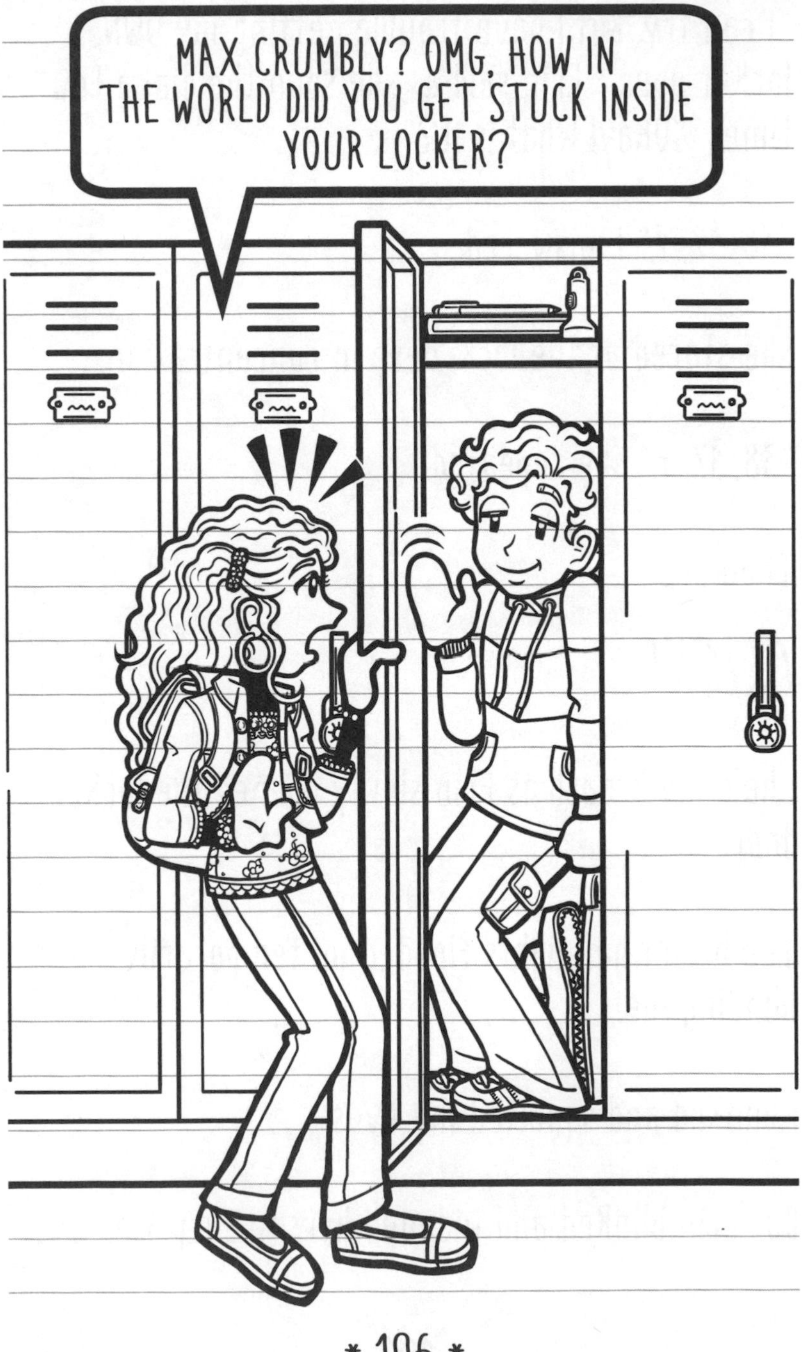
MAX CRUMBLY? OMG, HOW IN THE WORLD DID YOU GET STUCK INSIDE YOUR LOCKER?

I flushed with embarrassment.

"Um . . . would you believe by . . . accident?"

"By accident?! But, HOW?"

"Well, I was looking for my, um . . . math book, and I leaned over and fell in, and, um . . . somehow the door slammed closed and I ended up trapped inside. That's exactly what happened. Kind of . . ."

Erin just stared at me in disbelief like I had a two-pound booger dangling out of my nose.

"Oh, really? Puh-leeze, Max! You actually expect me to believe that?"

Then she rolled her eyes at me so hard, I thought they were going to pop out and roll down the hall.

"Look, I don't mean to get into your business, but if someone did this to you, you owe it to yourself to report them. If NOT, lurking inside your locker like some kind of creepy, freaky . . .

locker vampire could be dangerous! I suggest you get some psychiatric help. FAST! At least maybe talk to the school counselor or someone. I really need to get going. I think I left something in the library, and my parents are going to have a meltdown if I don't find it. Bye."

She turned and rushed down the hall.

"Erin, wait! I, um . . . just wanted to let you know that I'm still willing to help out with your play. I can stay after school next week. And I paint really fast, so . . ."

Erin stopped and spun around to face me.

"Thanks, Max. But the play . . . it got, um . . . canceled," she answered, and stared at the floor.

"Oh, I didn't know! I'm really sorry to hear that," I muttered, wanting to kick myself.

"Hey, I gave it my best shot. Besides, there's always next year." She shrugged. "I guess I owe you an apology for the way I acted. I had just gotten the bad news from my advisor and was a little upset. But still, that's no excuse."

"No problem at all." I smiled. "I was just trying to help."

Then we both just kind of stood there, looking at each other and not saying anything.

AWKWARD!!

I was about to mention the fact that I was seriously thinking about joining the computer club, when Erin finally broke the silence.

"Well, be careful! And don't go accidentally falling into any more lockers. Because, dude, that's just BEYOND WEIRD. See you."

I watched as she disappeared down the hall.

Did Erin just call me . . .

BEYOND WEIRD?!!

Yep! She DID!

Okay, so why did I suddenly feel like crawling BACK into my locker and slamming the door?

I sighed and grabbed my backpack.

As I looked at the clock near the main office a new sense of dread spread over me, and my stomach started to churn.

I had gotten to school twenty minutes late and had been stuck in my locker for almost twenty minutes, which meant I had missed most of my first-hour math class.

I didn't have a choice but to drag my butt back to the office and request a SECOND slip.

For being even MORE tardy! . . .

ME, GETTING A SECOND TARDY SLIP!

And since I'd probably already missed our math quiz, I was going to get an F and a note home to my parents.

Which wasn't quite as horrible as the fact that Erin, the ONLY person in the entire school who'd even bothered to talk to me in the past two weeks (well . . . other than Thug), thought I was some kind of psychotic LOCKER VAMPIRE WEIRDO.

I hated to admit it, but maybe Erin was right about talking to someone about my Thug Thurston problem.

And since I was already in the office, I could just skip my science class and ask to see Ms. Robinson, the school counselor.

After I explained what happened to me this morning at school, she'd probably give me an excused pass AND authorization to make up my math quiz.

Everything would work out just fine!

UNTIL Thug found out that I'd RATTED on him!!

And BROKE BOTH MY ARMS!

The last thing I needed was for my parents to pull me out of middle school to be homeschooled by Grandma until I graduated from high school.

Suddenly, being stuck in my locker seemed like the LEAST of my problems.

The first class period wasn't even over yet!

And my day was ~~already in the TOILET!~~ NOT going well!

12. SETUP FOR A LOCKDOWN?

Lucky for me, I somehow managed to steer clear of Thug the ENTIRE rest of the day.

WHEW!!

So when the last bell finally rang at three o'clock, I decided the best way to avoid a run-in with him after school would be to hide out in the new computer lab for fifteen minutes.

Our brand-new computer lab just opened two weeks ago, and it's my favorite place to hang out.

It has that weird new-computer smell that only computer nerds can truly appreciate.

After three years and a dozen fund-raisers, the school purchased $100,000 worth of equipment.

But the best part is, I've NEVER seen Thug in there. EVER! I was chillaxing and having a blast playing Valiant Knights of the Galaxy. . . .

ME, PLAYING VIDEO GAMES IN
THE NEW COMPUTER LAB

So when my watch suddenly beeped at four p.m., I was surprised that I'd been playing an entire hour!

It was eerily quiet, and no one was around. Even the computer lab teacher had cleared out.

FINALLY!

It was safe to make my escape and head home. I was SUPER happy that we had a three-day weekend.

And the icing on the cake was that there would be no Thug Thurston for an entire seventy-two hours!! WOO-HOO!

But, most importantly, I was relieved that I'd managed to SURVIVE yet another WEEK at school with Thug.

All while successfully AVOIDING another school year being homeschooled with Grandma. SWEET!! Right?!

Yep! Max C. had once again outsmarted Thug T.!

I did my VICTORY DANCE. . . .

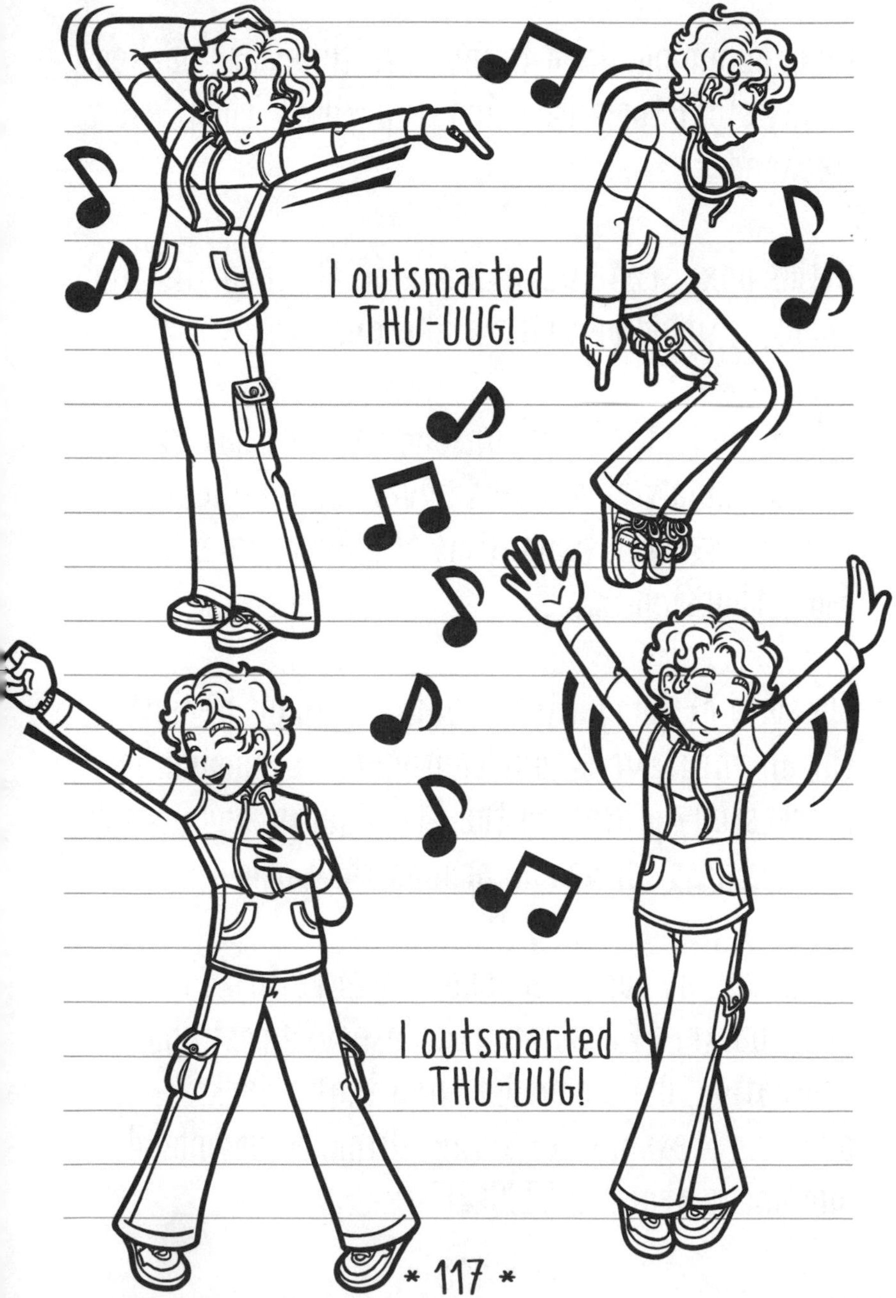
I outsmarted THU-UUG!
I outsmarted THU-UUG!

Then I moonwalked all the way back to my locker.

I was humming along to my fave tunes as I packed up my stuff for a relaxing, fun-filled, Thug-less weekend.

If this next scene were in one of my favorite comic books, it would be written like this. . . .

"When we last left our unsung hero, he had used his extremely high IQ and advanced intelligence to completely outsmart his evil archnemesis, Thug Thurston.

"In spite of doing intense battle with his nemesis for an entire week, our courageous champion has successfully protected the life, liberty, and pursuit of happiness for people around the world.

"However, as our hero prepares to return to headquarters for some well-deserved rest and relaxation, little does he know that a dark, ominous presence has slowly slithered up behind him and is about to STRIKE!"

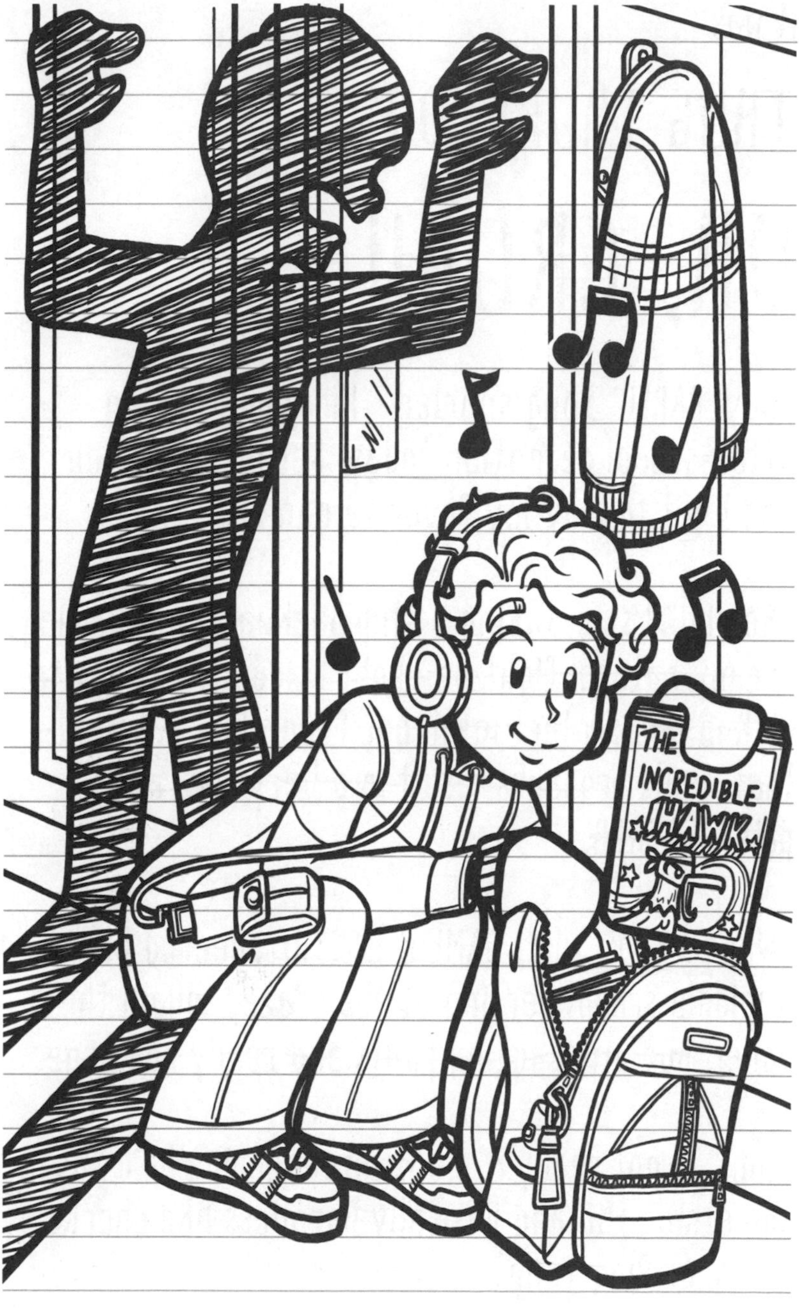
THE INCREDIBLE HAWK

It was . . .

THUG THURSTON?!

OH, CRUD!!

"Hey, BARF!" Thug snarled. "I'm glad I had an after-school detention today. Because now you and I get to play my favorite game!"

"Really!" I said, taking a step backward ~~and waiting for my natural fight-or-flight bladder response to kick in and protect me from Thug's BRUTAL game that would probably result in a very slow and painful DEATH~~.

"Wanna know what GAME it is?" He sneered like a middle school version of the crazed villain the Joker, ~~but with sagging pants and really bad acne~~.

"Um . . . not really?" I answered, hoping he'd say something fun and basically harmless like checkers, chess, or Ping-Pong.

And if I was REALLY lucky, Thug was into my little brother's favorite game, Duck, Duck, Goose!

"It's called LOCK-A-LOSER-IN-A-LOCKER! And today YOU'RE the loser!" Thug jeered.

"That doesn't sound very fun," I muttered.

"Well, it's FUN for ME!!" He grinned like a shark.

That's when I began to struggle with some very serious and troubling questions.

WHERE was my nervous bladder when I REALLY, REALLY needed it?!

And WHY had every other human being been given the FIGHT-or-FLIGHT instinct to survive, when I had been CURSED with, um . . .

PANIC-and-PEE?

I quickly grabbed my backpack and tried to make a mad dash for the exit.

But Thug grabbed me by my shirt, picked me up off the ground, and tossed me into my locker!

Then he slammed the door.

BAM!!

"NOOOOO!!" I screamed from inside.

"Have a nice WEEKEND, BARF!!" He laughed as his footsteps echoed down the hall.

I could NOT believe all of this was happening to me AGAIN!!

Only this was ten times WORSE!

All the students and teachers were gone.

And it appeared that most of the other faculty and staff had already left as well.

Suddenly my heart started to pound, and I broke into a cold sweat!

The warm, musty air inside my locker was already making it hard for me to breathe.

But I hadn't given up!

YET!!

Sorry, Thug!

But Max Crumbly wasn't going down without a fight!

Mustering all of my strength, I frantically kicked the door and yelled at the top of my lungs as my cold, harsh reality slowly sank in. . . .

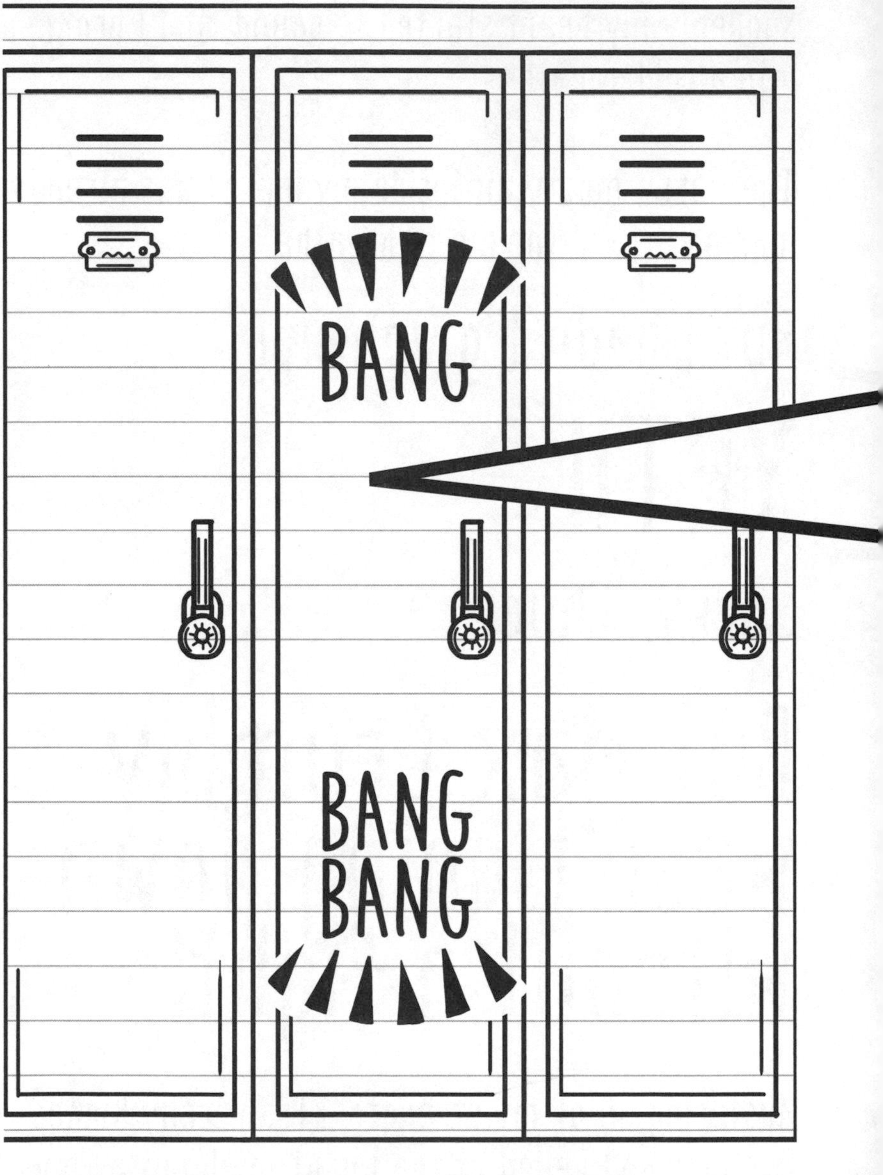
BANG
BANG
BANG

I WAS STUCK IN MY LOCKER . . .

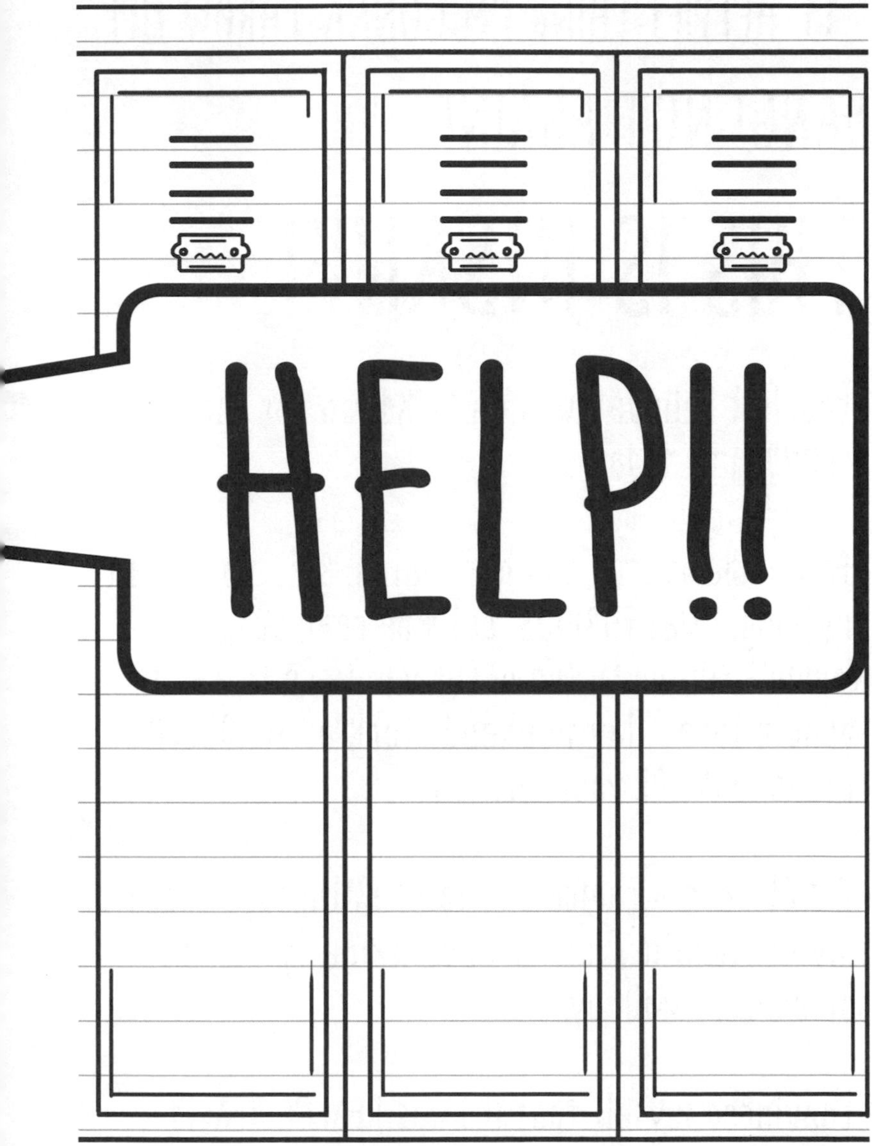
HELP!!

. . . FOR A THREE-DAY WEEKEND!!

13. HELP!! I THINK I'M GONNA THROW UP!

DANG! NOT AGAIN!

THIS IS INSANE!

I couldn't believe I was on lockdown for the SECOND time today!

I felt embarrassed and humiliated. But, more than anything, I was FURIOUS. Let's be real, people. Wouldn't YOU be ticked off if you were forced to spend a three-day weekend stuck at SCHOOL?!! Let alone INSIDE your locker?!

I didn't have a choice but to peek through those tiny vents in my locker and anxiously wait for someone to walk by.

I convinced myself that if I was REALLY, REALLY patient, at some point a random person would wander down the hall and rescue me.

But, unfortunately, no random wanderer passed by.

Then I told myself that even though it was a three-day weekend and mostly EVERYONE was already gone, there was STILL a SLIGHT chance SOMEONE had hung around after school. And THAT person would rescue me.

But sadly, no after-school hang-arounder appeared.

That's when I gathered every ounce of courage and bravely confronted my very difficult situation. . . .

~~My nervous bladder was acting up again, and if I didn't get out of that DANG locker soon, I was going to PEE my pants!~~

My life was completely over, and I was going to DIE a lonely, painful, and senseless DEATH!

TRAPPED within the four metal walls of my locker. Like a disgusting, stinky . . . human-sized, um . . .

SARDINE in a ... CAN!!

ME, TRAPPED LIKE A SARDINE
INSIDE MY LOCKER!

But do you wanna know what's even MORE disgusting?!

My grandma loves to mash up sardines with Cheez Whiz and Ketchup and eat them on crackers.

BLURP! That was me throwing up inside my mouth.

After what seemed like FOREVER, my watch beeped at six p.m., and I realized I'd been stuck in my locker for almost TWO. Whole. Hours.

I was starting to feel . . . **HOPELESS!**

That's when I had yet ANOTHER panic attack and used my inhaler for the second time today.

Needless to say, after THAT little episode I was anxious, exhausted, and dripping with sweat.

I also felt really dizzy and queasy.

But don't get it twisted!

A combination of extreme stress, exhaustion, heat, and dehydration is enough to make even a superhero feel SICK!

HOW do I know this?

Because the same thing happened in THE INCREDIBLE HAWK (my very own comic book series that I write in my spare time).

Although he's a humble part-time forest ranger, race car driver, and rock star, he has an amazing superpower, to turn into an indestructible screeching hawk just by screaming, "BAH-KAAW!! BAH-KAAW!! BAH-KAAAAAAW!"

And get this!

In Volume 3 the Incredible Hawk actually puked up two lizards, three squirrels, and eleven mice while doing battle with his archnemesis, ~~Thug~~ the VENOMOUS VULTURE, in the Sahara Desert in 117-degree heat (which, I'm guessing, is probably the temperature inside my locker)!! . . .

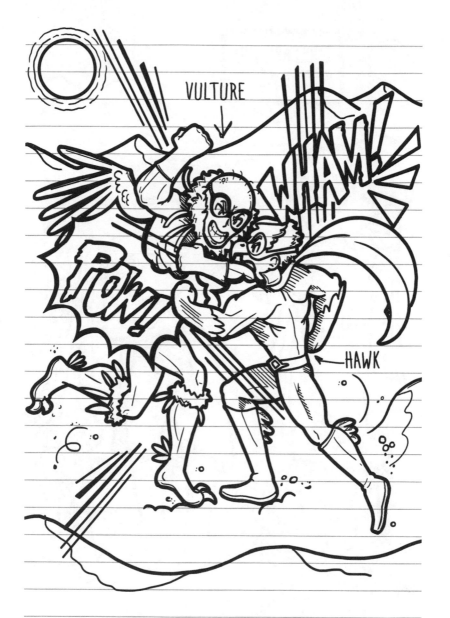

THE HAWK AND THE VULTURE
BATTLING IN THE DESERT!!

* 131 *

THE HAWK, LOSING HIS LUNCH!!

Hey, that scene was SICK in more ways than one.

There's no doubt the Incredible Hawk would make a KICK-BUTT superhero movie!! Right?!

Anyway, I was about to give up hope ~~and VOMIT~~ when I thought I heard a very faint sound....

SQUEAKY-SQUEAK! SQUEAKY-SQUEAK!
SQUEAKY-SQUEAK! SQUEAKY-SQUEAK!

I desperately peeked through the tiny vents in my locker and completely FREAKED!

~~I could NOT believe what I saw!~~

I could NOT believe what I THOUGHT I saw!

If you've ever been trapped in a place where you can barely SEE anything or HEAR anything, after a while your brain starts weirding out. Then your imagination takes over and you think, see, and hear some pretty WACKY STUFF.

SQUEAKY-SQUEAK! SQUEAKY-SQUEAK!

It's called SENSORY DEPRIVATION, my friends, and let me tell you . . . it is NOT fun.

I was ALSO a little worried about my brain cells dying off from some obscure and very deadly disease like . . . um . . .

LOCKER-ITIS!!

Hey, don't laugh. It could happen.

SQUEAKY-SQUEAK!
SQUEAKY-SQUEAK!

Anyway, there was a VERY good chance my mind was playing tricks on me and everything I'd just seen and heard in the hallway was merely a HALLUCINATION.

A very CRUEL and TWISTED one.

14. THE KING OF CLEAN ROCKS?!

If my life were a comic book, my situation would be summarized like this....

"When we last left our hero, he was trapped inside the four impenetrable walls of his locker, brutally imprisoned for three long days, or very possibly all of eternity, by his evil archnemesis, Thug Thurston! Will our courageous hero make it out alive? Or will he be EATEN like a helpless SARDINE with Cheez Whiz and Ketchup on the cold, hard CRACKER of DOOM?!"

I cowered in fear as a dark, phantom-like figure moved slowly down the hall toward my locker. And even though its shadow was massive, it made an unusually ~~annoying, but vaguely familiar,~~ high-pitched sound.

I didn't have the slightest idea WHO or WHAT it was. As its shadow fell upon my locker, I held my breath and cautiously peeked out.

That's when I saw ...

SQUEAKY-SQUEAK

A SCHOOL JANITOR?!

Since it was so late, I assumed he was finishing up his work and about to head home.

That's when I started yelling like a maniac. "HELP!! HELP!! PLEASE!! I'M STUCK INSIDE MY LOCKER, AND I CAN'T GET OUT. IT'S KIND OF AN EMERGENCY! HEEEEEEEELLP!"

The janitor stopped in his tracks, cocked his head, and just stared.

He appeared to be trying to figure out which locker the cries for help were coming from.

FINALLY! I'm going to be rescued!!

I was SO happy and SO relieved, I wanted to do my victory dance right there inside my locker. I never thought in a million years that a school janitor would end up saving my life.

I didn't know him that well. But I DID know he had a really tough job.

I mean, would YOU want to clean up vomit, unclog toilets, peel gooey wads of toilet paper off the bathroom ceilings, scrape gum from under desks, and do other assorted totally disgusting tasks?

EVERY SINGLE DAY for thirty years?

For a bunch of loud and obnoxious middle school kids?

I didn't think so!

No wonder the guy was always so GRUMPY!!

In spite of my personal problems, I suddenly felt GRATEFUL to be alive.

But mostly I was grateful I didn't have to clean up after 750 NASTY middle school students!

"UM . . . THANK YOU!! THANK YOU SO MUCH!!" I yelled through my locker. "I WAS STARTING TO THINK THAT I'D NEVER GET OUT OF HERE!"

The janitor nodded his head and then picked up his mop.

WHAT?! Was this guy going to try to pry my locker open with the mop handle or something?!

"EXCUSE ME, BUT I CAN GIVE YOU THE LOCKER COMBO. THAT WOULD BE A LOT EASIER THAN USING YOUR MOP!" I said.

Then he did the strangest thing.

He actually started to . . .

DANCE?!!

Listen, I was super happy about getting out of the locker too.

But I couldn't help thinking . . .

DUDE!! Let's save the VICTORY DANCE until AFTER you rescue me! Okay?!

Then things took a very TRAGIC turn!!

I finally noticed that the janitor was wearing . . .

AN MP3 PLAYER AND EARBUDS?!!

"NOOOOOOOO!!! HE CAN'T HEAR ME!!" I groaned and kicked my locker door in frustration.

The janitor didn't have the SLIGHTEST idea I was just inches away from him.

I could have just reached through the locker vents and SMACKED him (well, if I had, like, really teeny-tiny hands)!

And thanks to the VERY loud music he was blasting, it was going to be IMPOSSIBLE to get his attention.

Unless I maybe set my math book on FIRE and hoped he noticed the SMOKE billowing out of my locker.

It didn't take long for me to realize there was one thing WORSE than being trapped in my locker. . . .

Being trapped in my locker while being FORCED
to watch a school janitor dance while singing
off-key.

Sorry, but the guy was so bad, he couldn't carry
a tune in his mop bucket.

But since I was a captive audience, all I could do was
cringe while he sang and played air guitar on his
mop handle.

It was surreal!

He was like some kind of delusional geriatric rock
star on his farewell world tour . . .

THE
KING OF CLEAN
ROCKS!!

Then, in the middle of his song, he played a super-intense air guitar solo for three minutes.

Next he hopped down the hall like a 170-pound bunny on steroids. . . .

And for his finale he ran, dropped to his knees, and slid twenty feet down the hall. . . .

...dramatically ending his song with a fist pump
right back in front of (you guessed it) . . . MY LOCKER.

Talk about CRUEL IRONY! DANG!!

But, singing aside, I had to admit he put on one HECK of a show!

For an old dude with a mop, anyway.

I would have enjoyed it a lot better if I hadn't been watching it from, you know . . .

INSIDE OF MY STUPID LOCKER!!

After bowing to his thousands of imaginary fans, the janitor pushed his cart into a closet and started turning off all the lights in the building.

Then he danced down the hallway, past my locker, and right out the side exit door.

I know!

My REALLY bad day was getting WORSE by the minute.

Because NOW I was locked inside a DARK and CREEPY school building . . .

Alone.

While trapped INSIDE my locker.

With no food.

No water.

And no bathroom.

For an entire three-day weekend.

Sorry, but that was just WRONG on so many levels!

15. RANTINGS OF A LOCKER LUNATIC

Being trapped in my locker gave me plenty of time to do some serious thinking about my cruddy life.

Like, what was GOOD about it (my family, I guess) and what was BAD (I had a long list of stuff), and whether I had the power to change anything.

I was sick and tired of Thug treating me like DIRT. But, I had to admit, it was MY fault for letting him get away with it. I should've asked for help. I promised myself that IF I got out of this fiasco alive, I would NEVER, EVER let this happen to me again. Or to anyone else, for that matter.

I didn't deserve this! NOBODY deserved this! I felt really sad when I thought about my parents. They worried about me a lot and always asked how things were going at school. But I'd lied to them.

So NOW I'm going to tell them the TRUTH.

Dear Mom and Dad, THIS is how I'm FEELING! . . .

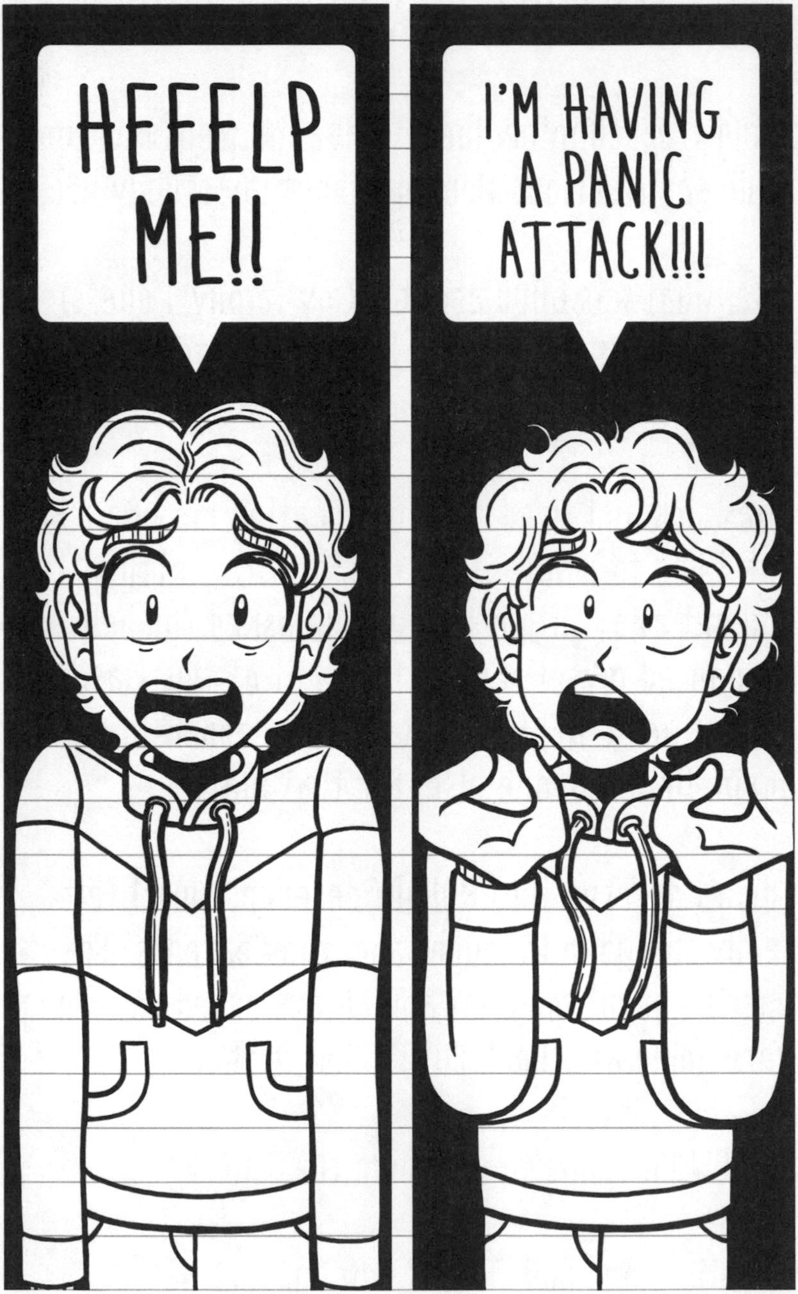
HEEELP ME!!
I'M HAVING A PANIC ATTACK!!!

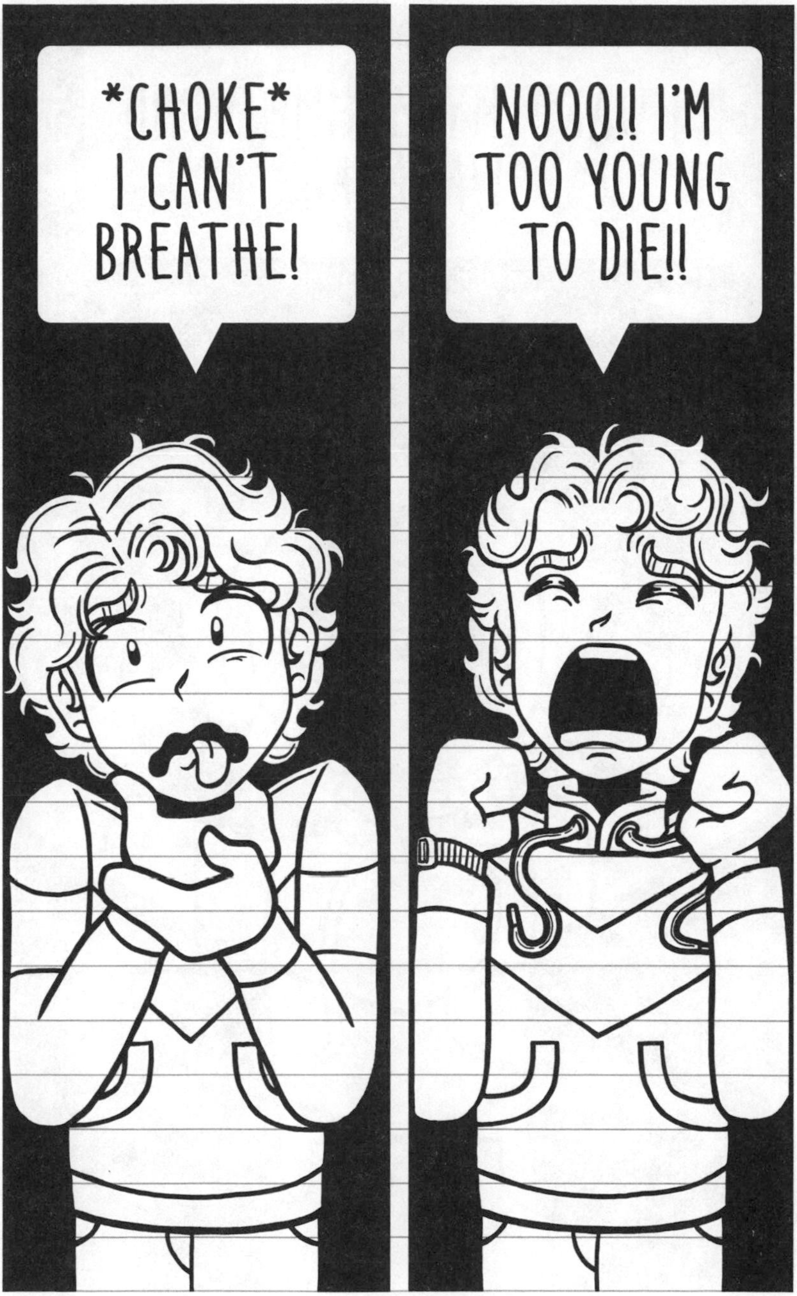
CHOKE I CAN'T BREATHE!
NOOO!! I'M TOO YOUNG TO DIE!!

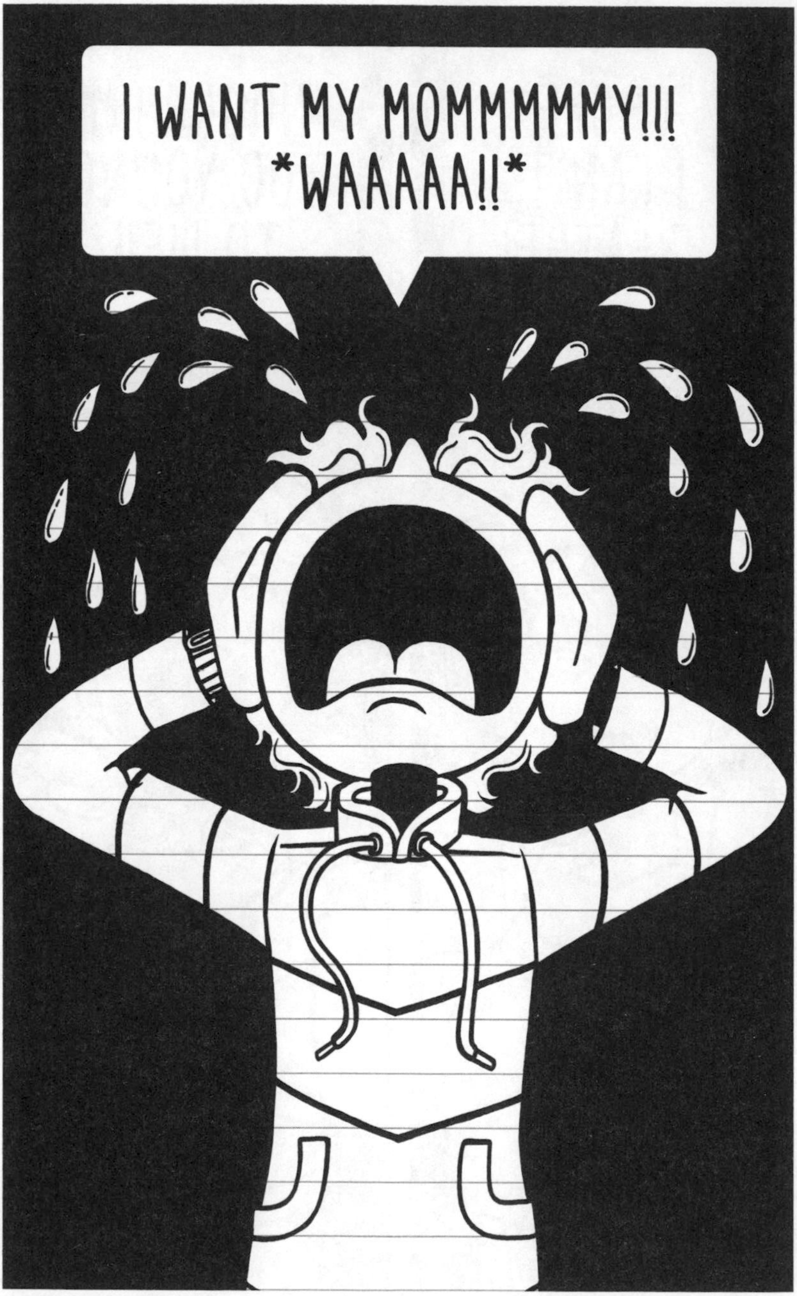
I WANT MY MOMMMMMY!!!
WAAAAA!!

Yeah, you could say my feelings are probably a little ~~overdramatic~~ intense and raw at the moment.

Sorry, but that's just where my head is right now.

It's about time everyone knew the truth.

Hey, there's no shame in MY game!

Anyway, I've been trapped in my locker now for over three hours. Which means I now have only . . .

Doing the math in my head

EIGHTY-FIVE MORE HOURS TO GO?!!

DANG!!

The worst part of all of this is that my family

won't even realize I'm MISSING until it's too late, due to my hectic schedule.

What outrageous, adrenaline-pumping, super-fun activities did I have planned for my three-day weekend?

How about rock climbing, a 5K race, extreme skiing, and a freestyle BMX competition!

NOT!!

My grandma planned to attend the annual Westchester Knitting Convention with her friends on Friday, Saturday, and Sunday to take a bunch of classes.

And get this!

She offered to pay me $20 a day to DOGSIT her mangy little mutt, Creampuff, at her house all weekend.

So, YES! I agreed to sleep over and babysit a mentally

disturbed dog with a nasty habit of scooting his butt on the carpet when he thinks no one is looking.

~~Which meant I'd mostly be eating, sleeping, watching TV, and playing video games for three whole days and actually getting PAID for it! SWEET!!~~

I bet you're probably thinking my grandma will just call my parents when I don't show up at her house.

Then my parents will call the police to report their darling child missing.

Then I'll be tracked down at my school and rescued all easy-peasy like! Right?

WRONG again!

This morning my grandma called me and CANCELED at the last minute.

~~But I'd decided NOT to mention this little detail to my parents since they'd been nagging me to clean out the garage and I was thinking about staying~~

~~overnight at Brandon's house and hanging out at~~
~~Fuzzy Friends all weekend instead.~~

My grandma and her friends decided NOT to
go to the knitting convention because the TV
weatherman predicted rain.

And although the convention was indoors, she said
the rain would aggravate her arthritis and make
her cankles swell, so she decided to stay home and
watch a *Golden Girls* marathon on TV instead.

And now my grandma thinks I'm at home with
my parents.

And my parents think I'm at my grandma's house.

Which means my ENTIRE FAMILY is blissfully
unaware of my whereabouts, although Megan
could not care less.

It will be several DAYS before they finally figure
out I'm in trouble and call the police.

And by that time it'll be too late!

Of course, Megan will celebrate my untimely death by turning my bedroom into the walk-in shoe closet she's always wanted.

And Oliver will put on his Bat Kid costume and gleefully scribble with black markers all over my personal stuff (including my cherished comic book collection) AND my bedroom walls, until he runs out of markers or drops from exhaustion, whichever occurs first.

I don't mean to be all doom and gloom, but short of a miracle, there's NO WAY I'm going to make it out of my locker ALIVE!

16. WHO SAYS A ZOMBIE CAN'T RAP?!

BEEP-BEEP! BEEP-BEEP!
BEEP-BEEP! BEEP-BEEP! BEEP!

My eyes fluttered open and my heart pounded like a bass drum as I was startled awake from a deep sleep.

The fog began to clear in my brain, and I realized my watch had just beeped 9:00 p.m. But for some reason it seemed a lot later than that.

My bedroom was a lot darker than usual too. Did I need a new bulb in my night-light?

My throat felt raw and my legs were cramping. Actually, my ENTIRE body ached.

And I'd just had the CRAZIEST dream!!

About . . . THUG THURSTON?!!

I leaned over to turn on the lamp sitting on my nightstand and . . .

BANG!!!

I hit my head against cold, hard metal.

OW!! That HURT! It felt like someone had rung a bell inside my brain.

"WHERE the heck am I?" I wondered.

I reached into the darkness and felt my coat, my backpack, my journal, and . . .

FOUR METAL WALLS?!

Suddenly all the memories came flooding back to me.

After school. Thug. Locker. Darkness. Janitor. Mop. More darkness . . .

THREE-DAY WEEKEND!

"NOOOOO!!!" I moaned. "Please let this be just a NIGHTMARE!"

But it WASN'T a bad dream. It was my REALITY. I was STILL trapped inside my locker and waiting to be rescued!!

UNLESS . . .

I closed my eyes and considered a horribly morbid thought.

Could I possibly . . . already be . . . DEAD?!

Sure, I felt a little achy, but I didn't feel . . . dead.

Although, I couldn't be sure, since I'd never been, you know, dead before.

I shifted into a more comfortable position and then wiggled my toes to help relieve the intense cramping in my legs.

Actually, muscle cramps were a very bad sign.

I'd read somewhere that a corpse could have a weird, intense muscle spasm and suddenly sit straight up.

YIKES!! Like, how FREAKY would THAT be at your great-grandaunt's funeral?! But HOW could I be dead when I still felt so . . . ALIVE?!

UNLESS . . .

I had an even MORE horribly morbid thought as chills ran down my spine.

What if I had already DIED inside my locker and come back as a . . .

ZOMBIE?!!

NOOOOOO!! (I was NOT happy about this!)

Well, one thing was for sure. Being UNDEAD was definitely NOT going to help my nonexistent social life or improve my really CRUDDY rep. . . .

ME, AS A ZOMBIE, HAVING LUNCH
IN THE SCHOOL CAFETERIA

I've seen the *ZOMBIE APOCALYPSE* movies 1, 2, 3, 4, 5, 6, and 7. And, basically, zombies are just mean, ugly, rotten people. No pun intended.

That's when I had to ask myself a really deep, philosophical question.

Do I STILL need to worry about Thug actually KILLING me if I'm a ZOMBIE and I'm ALREADY dead?

NOPE!! SWEET!

Which meant the next time Thug rolled up on me, I wouldn't have to be worried about him knocking me into tomorrow.

And I'd finally be able to squash our beef once and for all.

HOW?

I'd simply rip off a body part that I don't really need (like an ear or a thumb) and just hand it to him ~~and watch him totally FREAK!!~~ . . .

ME, AS ZOMBIE MAX,
SQUASHING THE BEEF WITH THUG!

Maybe my life as a zombie wouldn't be so bad after all. I was so inspired I decided to write a rap:

* *

MESSAGE FROM A MIDDLE SCHOOL ZOMBIE

I'm a zombie rapper, as you can see,
cursed to rock the mic for all eternity.

Although I'm undead, my rhymes are hot,
because unlike my corpse, my skills don't rot.

So don't be skurd. Don't tremble and shake.
Yes, I eat human flesh like it's birthday cake.

My eyes are sunken. My heart is like stone.
But I ONLY commit MURDER on the microphone!

My swagger is huge! My ego is chunky!
And my rotting smell? No joke, it's funky!

But the girls still love me! They scream and cry,
"OMG! It's a zombie! I'm too CUTE to DIE!"

Flies buzz all around me, and I'm dribbling drool.
But believing in myself is what makes ME cool!

Fitting in with the crowd was my only crave
in the life that I had before my cold, dark grave.

Listen up! If you seek, then you will find
YOU possess power that'll BLOW your mind!

Be true to YOURSELF when life gets INSANE!
I didn't get this smart from just eating brains!

I'm Zombie Max! My words cut like a knife.
I'll SLAY you first! Then I'll give you LIFE!

* *

WHOA!! I think this rap is actually kind of deep.

Who would have thought this zombie stuff would be
so empowering?

Well, the GOOD news is that I'm pretty sure I'm NOT
a zombie. WHY?

Because I hadn't had anything to eat since lunchtime, I was practically starving and my stomach was growling like a T. rex.

But I wasn't craving HUMAN FLESH at all! All I could think about was a juicy burger and a hot, cheesy double-sausage pizza.

However, the BAD news was that I could now add DYING OF STARVATION to my long list of personal problems.

That's when I suddenly remembered . . . !!

I felt along the bottom of my locker until I hit the jackpot!

It was a small plastic bag with three stale gingersnap cookies my grandma had made for me the first day of school. Her cookies were always as hard as a rock and tasted like cinnamon-sprinkled hockey pucks.

I had just tossed them inside my locker only because I was too lazy to walk down the hall to the trash can twenty feet away.

Anyway, I snarfed down every last crumb of those doggy biscuits like they were my favorite warm, freshly baked double chocolate chip cookies.

Dude! These were the best NASTY-TASTING cookies I'd ever eaten in my ENTIRE life!

Thanks to my little nap and not-so-yummy snack, I had a burst of energy and optimism.

Maybe there was a way out of my locker after all.

I just had to find it. AND FAST!

Apparently, I WASN'T a half-rotted ZOMBIE (yet, anyway)!

But I'd been cooped up in my hot, stuffy locker for so long that I was definitely starting to SMELL like one. FOR REAL!

17. JUST KICKIN' IT!

I turned on my flashlight and carefully examined every single square inch of my locker.

The door and two side walls were made of heavy-duty sheet metal held together with screws and brackets.

However, the back wall panel was fairly thin.

This made sense, since the lockers were up against a wall in the hallway.

That's when I excitedly came up with a brilliant plan! Escaping from my locker would be a PIECE OF CAKE and take me barely five minutes . . .

If ONLY I had the right POWER TOOLS!!

But, unfortunately, my mom HADN'T stuffed a blowtorch, electric screwdriver, and jackhammer into my backpack along with my PB and J sandwich. . . .

IF ONLY MOM HAD PACKED SOME
POWER TOOLS ALONG WITH MY LUNCH!!

Which meant that I was pretty much STUCK inside my locker for another . . .

Doing the math inside my head

EIGHTY-THREE MORE HOURS!

FOR REAL?!!!!!!

There was NO WAY I was going to last another eighty-three hours!

All my energy and optimism gushed out of me like air from a deflating balloon and was quickly replaced with anger and frustration.

That's when I totally lost it and kicked the back wall.

BAM!!!

I kicked it REALLY hard. Unfortunately, SO hard I was afraid I had broken my ding-dang foot.

OWWW!!!

That's when I heard a strange sound.

And NO! It WASN'T me sobbing from the intense pain in my foot. It was more like cracking and crumbling.

And NO! It wasn't the sound of broken and crushed bones in my foot, smarty-pants!

So I kicked it even harder with my other foot and then put my ear up against the back panel.

It sounded like old drywall crumbling and falling.

COULD THIS BE A WAY OUT OF MY LOCKER?!!!

With renewed hope, I kept kicking the back panel as hard as I could.

BAM! BAM! BAM!

Several screws popped loose from the side walls and dropped to the floor.

Even though I was sweating like a pig and both of my feet throbbed with pain, I kept at it.

BAM! BAM! BAM!

I kicked that panel like it was Thug's BUTT!!

BAM! BAM! BAM!

Finally, I heard a loud . . .

SNAP! CRACK! CRASH!

Exhausted and breathing heavily, I leaned against a side wall and examined the back panel with my flashlight.

There must have been a water pipe leaking nearby, because damp, rotted drywall had crumbled away.

Small chunks of it lay on the floor of my locker like lopsided snowballs.

The back panel was still partially attached by several screws along its top edge.

However, now it was literally swinging back and forth like a giant doggy door.

I grabbed the panel and pulled it behind me.

Then I carefully leaned forward to take a closer look at the damaged wall.

My mind was completely blown by what I saw. . . .

A HUGE HOLE!!

But here's the CREEPY part! A mysterious RED GLOW was coming from somewhere on the other side!

Okay, I'll admit that I felt ~~so completely terrified that I wanted to fall on the floor and roll around while hysterically screaming my head off!!~~ a little nervous.

It gave me a really bad vibe, like I was about to enter a HORROR MOVIE or something.

But don't get it twisted!

I like WATCHING those movies, NOT actually becoming one of the clueless murder victims.

So I had to make a tough decision.

I could turn back and go wait inside my locker for another (*doing the math in my head*) EIGHTY-TWO-POINT-FIVE HOURS until I was rescued, or crawl through that hole into the possibly freaky unknown.

It's always easier to ignore a problem and do nothing because you're scared out of your mind.

But that was EXACTLY how I'd gotten myself into this huge mess to begin with.

Sorry, but I was sick and tired of living like that.

I decided to take my chances with the hole in the wall!

I didn't have the slightest idea WHERE it would take me.

And I didn't really care.

All I wanted were TWO things:

First, a BATHROOM!

And second, an EXIT DOOR! So I could get the HECK outta, um ... wherever I was ... and go HOME!!

18. I ENTER THE DEEP, DARK BOWELS OF . . . WHERE AM I?!

I wanted to travel lightly, so I decided to leave my backpack and textbooks inside my locker.

I grabbed my inhaler and flashlight and stuffed them in my pants pocket. Then I stuck my journal inside the front pocket of my sweatshirt.

When I stared out at the strange red glow for the second time, I noticed that the room looked almost smoky from the large amount of dust that had been stirred up by the falling drywall.

But as the dust began to settle, I saw an old red emergency lightbulb dimly flickering a few feet above my head. It created strange moving shadows that slowly circled around me like evil dancing ghosts waiting for the right moment to attack. GULP!!

I shuddered and broke into a cold sweat. Suddenly I had a renewed appreciation for my safe, warm, and cozy locker. (I know, I can't believe I just said that either!)

When the dust finally settled, I realized I was inside a strange room that looked like it had been closed off from the school for decades.

Dust and cobwebs covered everything, while several leaks from the ceiling dripped off pipes and made black puddles of water on the floor. It smelled more damp and musty than the boys' showers after we'd run the mile in PE class.

On the right side of the room stood two humongous tanks connected to fat pipes that ran along most of the ceiling and walls.

Had I discovered the secret lair of a twelve-foot-tall robotic monster with a dozen octopus-like arms?!

On the left side of the room was a pile of rotted drywall (okay, THAT was my fault!), a tall metal ladder, and even more pipes. It looked like I had stumbled upon an old boiler room that had been used to heat the school back in the day, except now it had a super-high creepiness factor. . . .

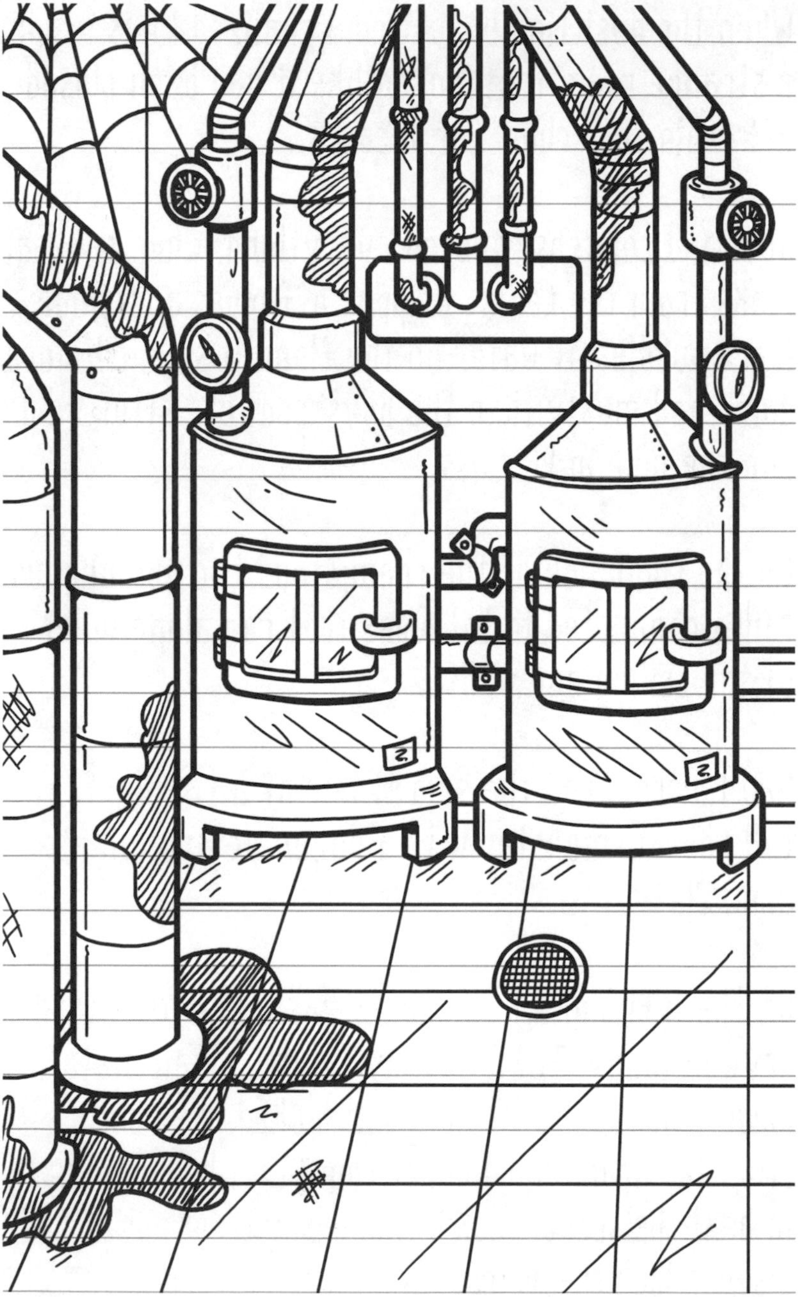

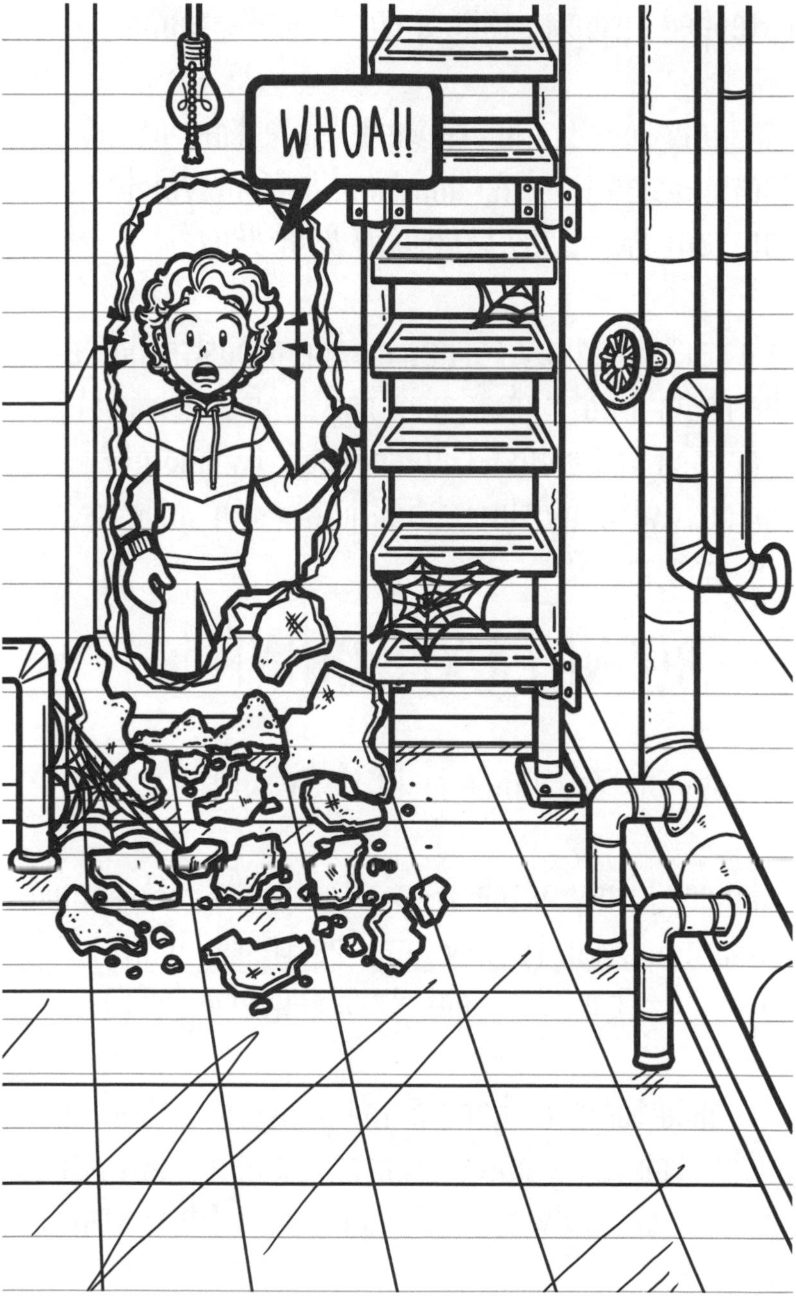
WHOA!!

I stepped inside to take a closer look around.

The only sounds I heard were the echoes of my footsteps on the tile floor and an annoyingly constant *DRIP-DRIP! DRIP-DRIP! DRIP-DRIP!*

In a dark, shadowy corner on the opposite side of the room, I noticed a large red door with a rusty doorknob and a dust-covered sign. I wiped off the dust with my sleeve and blinked in surprise. The sign said:

EMERGENCY EXIT ONLY!

I did my victory dance right there on the spot!

I glanced at my watch. If I walked really fast, I could make it home in twenty minutes. Which meant I still had time for a late-night pizza delivery! SWEET!

I grabbed the door handle and pulled it with all my might. The rusty hinges screeched like a wet cat as the door slooowly opened. I gasped and just stared in shock . . .

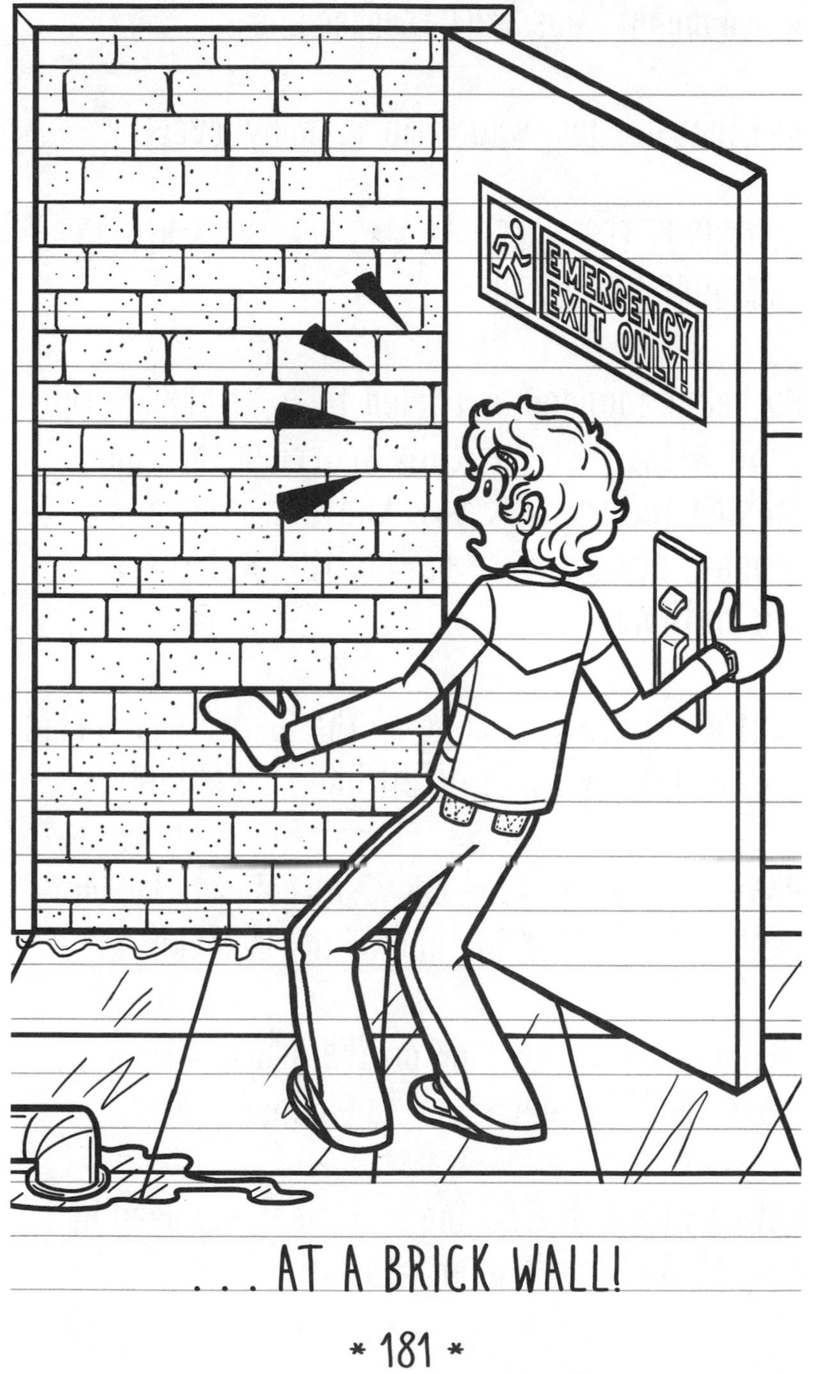
EMERGENCY
EXIT ONLY!

. . . AT A BRICK WALL!

Which meant I was STILL trapped!!

And that was just WRONG on so many levels.

WHY DID IT FEEL LIKE LIFE WAS PLAYING A REALLY SICK JOKE ON ME??!!

My heart pounded as I tried to fight off another panic attack. I frantically searched the room, looking for any way out. Another door, a window, even a loose ceiling tile! But there was nothing.

I sat on the bottom rung of the ladder and buried my head in my hands. I felt like SCREAMING!

Okay, so NOW my dead body was going to be found in the BOILER ROOM instead of my LOCKER!!

Well, I could always look on the bright side. At least I had a bigger space to DIE in!

I stared up at the ceiling and shook my head in disgust. And that's when I saw it!

A WAY OUT!! . . .

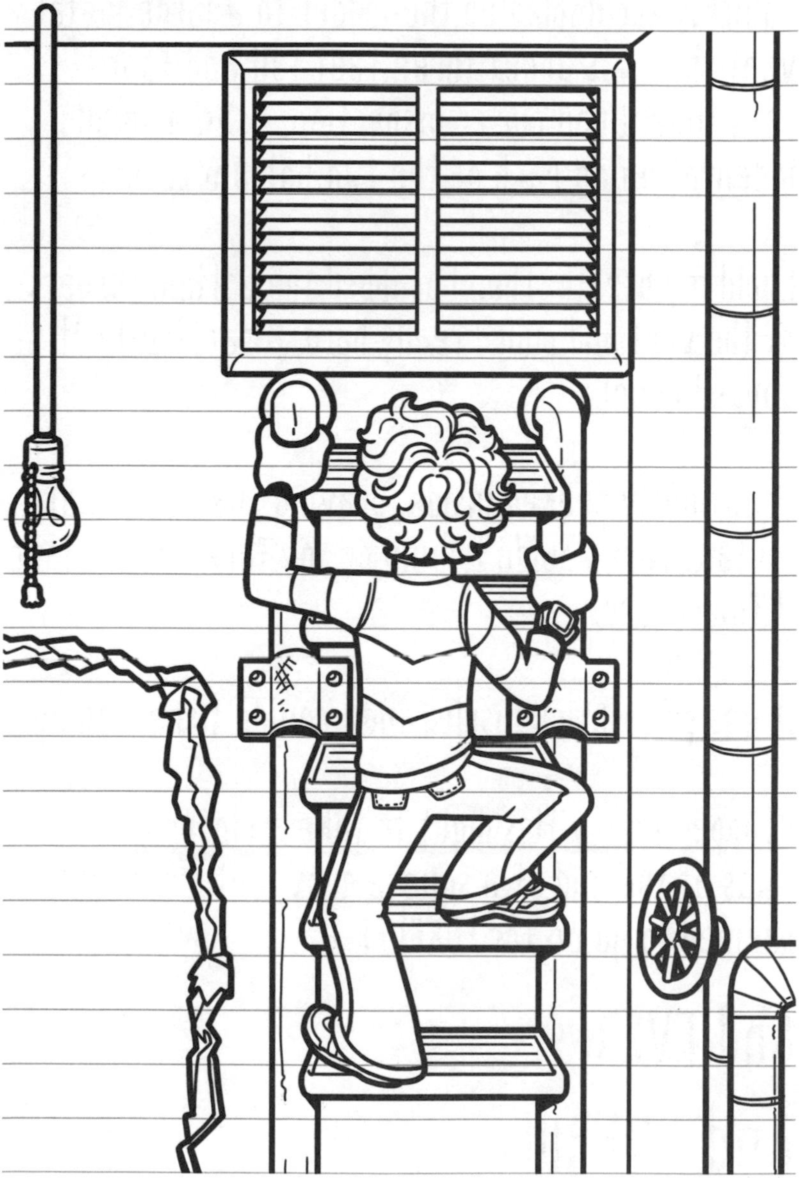

19. LORD OF THE LABYRINTH

I quickly scrambled up the ladder to a large metal vent that was about three feet tall and four feet wide. Upon closer inspection, I saw a small indentation on each of the two bottom corners.

I held my breath. Then I grabbed the bottom corners of the vent and pulled really hard. Miraculously, it popped open!

I cautiously peeked inside, praying that a pack of mutant rats wouldn't jump on my face and mistake it for cheese.

It was pitch-black inside, and I couldn't see a thing.

I flipped on my flashlight to take a closer look. I was at the end of a square gray metal tunnel that seemed to go on for FOREVER.

And EVER!

And EVER!!!

Based on all the movies I've seen, tunnels like this ALWAYS lead outside. PERFECT!!

Or to the roof. COOL!!

Or into a giant garbage Dumpster. EWWW!!

Or into a 1,200-degree scorching incinerator. AAAAAAAAAAAHHHHHHHHH!!!

Okay, on second thought, maybe this WASN'T such a good idea after all.

I sighed deeply and turned around to stare at the dank, musty boiler room and the jagged hole that led back to my dark, cramped locker.

Did I want to hang out here for the next (*doing the math in my head*) EIGHTY-TWO HOURS?!

Definitely NOT!!

I quickly hoisted myself up into the tunnel and crawled inside as the vent door slammed noisily behind me.

I slowly crawled through the tunnel, trying to ignore the sudden claustrophobic panic I was feeling. Yes, I was actually starting to miss my very spacious, dark, and dank boiler room!...

I hadn't seen any rats yet. But what if there were poisonous spiders? Or snakes? Or hungry ORCS?!

I was just about to turn around and head back, when the tunnel took a sharp left turn. . . .

That's when I spotted a dark rectangular shape about fifteen yards away.

I immediately froze.

What if it was a trapdoor to a chute that would send me plummeting headfirst fifty feet straight down into the school's, um . . . SEWAGE SYSTEM?!

I cautiously inched forward to take a closer look as my heart pounded in my chest.

Actually, it was another VENT!

Only this one was slightly smaller than the one in the boiler room.

I shined my flashlight on it and then squinted to see what was on the other side.

I was pleasantly surprised to see a classroom.

But it wasn't just ANY classroom. It was . . .

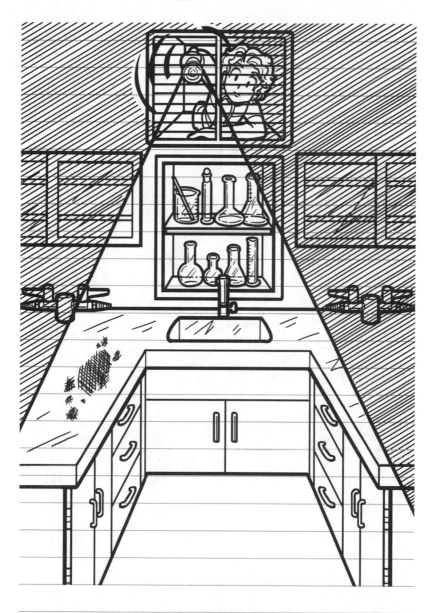

MY PHYSICAL SCIENCE CLASSROOM!

I even saw the burnt spot on the lab counter where, on the second day of school, Thug set his textbook on fire to IMPRESS his cute new lab partner. . . .

But, unfortunately, Thug's little fire spread from his book to her lab notes! Then from her lab notes to her purse!

The fire alarm went off and the sprinkler system came on, and soon four screaming fire trucks were speeding toward our school at seventy miles an hour.

It was **INSANE!!**

Thank goodness no one was hurt.

Of course, students were thrilled when school was dismissed and we were sent home for the rest of the day so the janitors could clean up.

I think Thug definitely should have gotten suspended for that little prank. But he swore it was all a big accident, and the principal gave him the benefit of the doubt.

I feel really sorry for Thug's lab partner. The poor girl was probably traumatized. I never saw her in our lab again, so I'm pretty sure she transferred to a different class. Or maybe even a different SCHOOL!

Anyway, I FINALLY figured out where I was. Inside the school's extensive ventilation system.

It's basically a mile of tunnels that run through the entire school, with vents inside every classroom, as well as the gym, cafeteria, teachers' lounge, office, and hallways.

It's pretty much an endless LABYRINTH!

SWEET! Right?! I felt like I was in my own virtual reality VIDEO GAME or something.

And I, MAXWELL CRUMBLY, was the mighty . . .

LORD OF THE LABYRINTH!

Anyway, I was in the eighth-grade hall and crawled past my art, English, and social studies classrooms.

But there was only ONE room I was anxious to visit before I headed for home.

Yep, the boys' bathroom!

And, judging from my current location inside the vents, I needed to go about forty yards beyond my social studies class, hang a right into the main hall, go twenty yards past the computer lab, and *BAM!*

Estimated time of arrival, two minutes and thirty seconds.

However, as I was approaching the computer lab, I noticed the strangest thing!

A light was on inside, and I could hear voices. It sounded like several adults.

Only, I couldn't imagine why teachers, or even janitors, would still be at the school so late on a three-day weekend.

My curiosity got the best of me, so I decided to investigate by taking a closer look.

I had no intention of blowing my cover and possibly risking a detention for being on school property after hours, even though I was actually there against my will.

Besides, it would be almost impossible for them to see me stealthily spying on them from way up inside the vent, right?!

Hey, what could possibly go wrong?!

20. DO THEY REALLY SERVE MIGHTY MEAT MONSTER PIZZA IN PRISON?

Okay, I'll admit I was a little FREAKED OUT! THERE WERE THREE MEN IN THE COMPUTER LAB!! At first I thought they were janitors. But soon it became quite obvious they weren't.

"This is it, boys! Our biggest heist yet," said a short, dumpy guy in a cheap green suit. He had ugly sideburns and a lopsided toupee ~~that looked like a very large and dirty groundhog had crawled on top of his head and DIED~~. "Time to graduate from amateur pickpockets to professional burglars."

"Now, THAT'S what I'm talking about, Ralph!" exclaimed a tall, skinny guy with a bandanna tied around his head. "I'm gonna buy a camera and a ton of new video games with my cut of the cash! Then I'm gonna quit my job flippin' burgers and post videos of me playing games on YouTube. I'll be a millionaire in no time!"

"Tucker, how are you gonna make money from

that?!" Ralph glared. "I know! Just ask complete strangers to send you twenty dollars in the mail and then sit back and watch the money pour in!"

Tucker scratched his head. "Um, actually, I hadn't figured it out yet. But your idea is genius! If I asked one million people to send me twenty dollars, I'd have, like, um . . . twenty million dollars, right?"

"WRONG!!" Ralph growled. "Because nobody would be STUPID enough to send an IDIOT like you money just 'cause you asked for it!"

"Speaking of stupid idea, can somebody tell me why we're at a SCHOOL?" asked a big muscular guy with spiked black hair, wearing a jean jacket. "What are we stealing, math books? You both know I failed math, right? I'm not that good with numbers! My favorite subject was lunch. I always got straight As in lunch. Actually, I'm really hungry right now. I could eat a horse!"

Were these guys serious? They seemed like characters from a Saturday-morning cartoon.

"Moose, you're ALWAYS whining about being hungry!" Tucker said. You're just a two-hundred-pound baby, dude!"

"Tucker, don't start with me . . . !" Moose shot back.

"Both of you, shut your TRAPS!" growled Ralph.

"Well, I think we should've robbed that Queasy Cheesy pizza place we passed on the way over here," Moose said. "If we'd used the drive-through window, we would've gotten the money in sixty seconds! And if they make you wait longer than that, you get a FREE cheese pizza! I saw the commercial on TV!"

"I saw that commercial too!" Tucker exclaimed. "And if you buy a ten-piece buffalo wings, you get an order of extra-spicy wings for FREE! Man, I LOVE extra-spicy wings!"

"Quit yapping about food and FOCUS!!" Ralph yelled angrily as his toupee flopped around on his head like it was trying to escape. "IF I WANTED TO HANG OUT WITH TWO CLOWNS, I WOULD HAVE GONE TO THE CIRCUS!!"

"Sorry, boss!" Moose and Tucker said glumly.

"Listen up! I'm going to explain this one LAST time," Ralph said through gritted teeth. "This school has thirty-six brand-new computers, each worth a small fortune! And there's no security. Do you know what that means?!"

"Are you kidding?!" Tucker said excitedly. "That means I can update my Facebook page from here! You should see the latest pictures I took of my cat, Mr. Fuzzybottoms! Yesterday was his birthday!"

"Forget your stupid CAT!" Moose grumbled. "Let's just get this job over with. I get cranky when I'm hungry! I just wish I'd brought a snack. I'm STARVING, guys!"

"Well, STARVE on your OWN time!" Ralph snarled. "You're on MY clock now. Start moving these computers into the hall!"

WHOA!! These guys were actually planning to STEAL all of the school's new COMPUTERS!! . . .

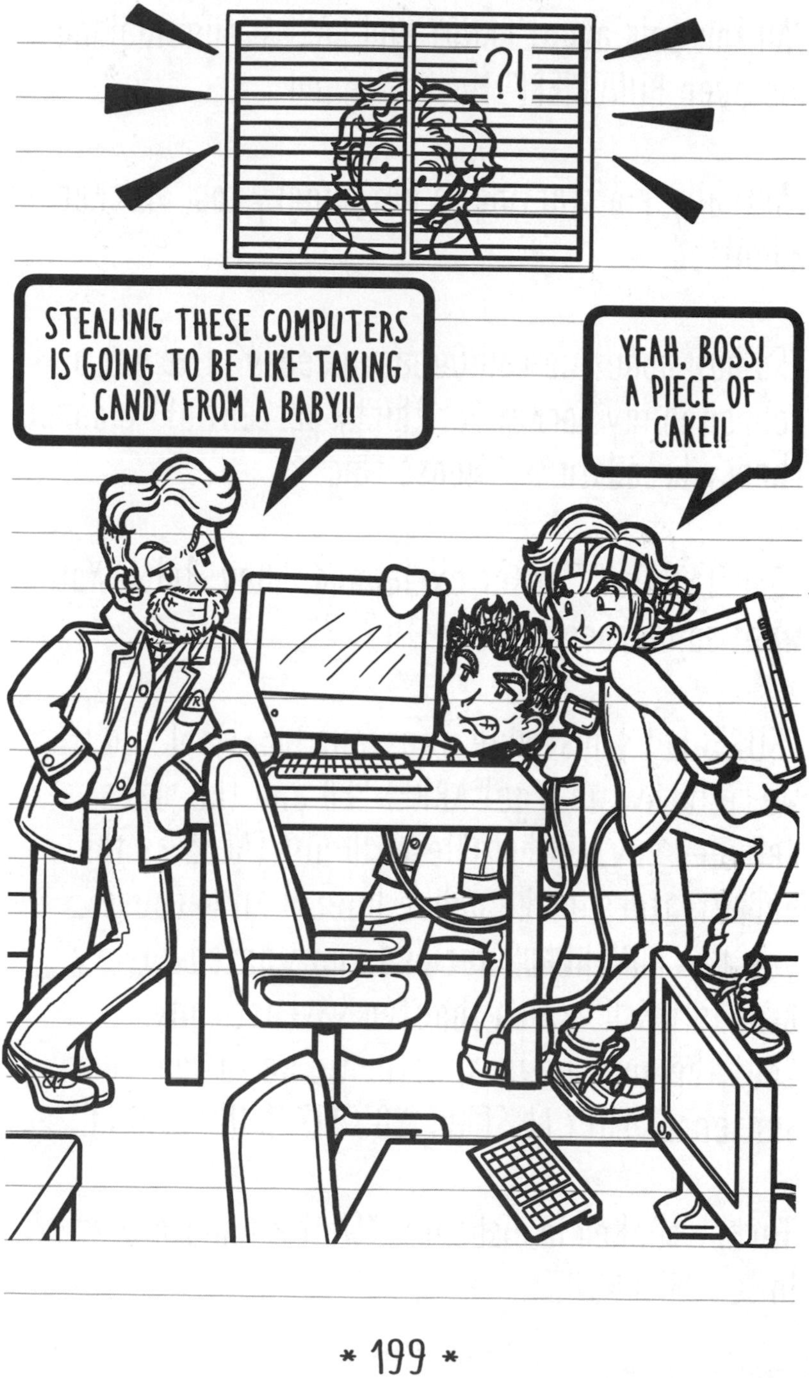
?!
STEALING THESE COMPUTERS IS GOING TO BE LIKE TAKING CANDY FROM A BABY!!
YEAH, BOSS! A PIECE OF CAKE!!

"All this talk about CANDY and CAKE is just making me even HUNGRIER!" Moose whined.

"Actually, I'm starting to get hungry too," Tucker admitted.

"So how about we call Queasy Cheesy? I've got a coupon in my pocket for thirty percent off a dozen cheesy breadsticks," Moose said.

"Dude! I'm in!" Tucker exclaimed. "Hey, Ralph! You want some cheesy breadsticks?"

"SURE! Let's just give away our location! And if we're lucky, we'll get ARRESTED and the pizza delivery guy will be able to ID our FACES as the perpetrators in the police lineup! All because you two BONEHEADS decided you wanted cheesy breadsticks!!" Ralph shouted sarcastically.
"But the good news is, after we get a ten-year sentence, THEY'LL SERVE YOU PIZZA IN PRISON!!!"

Tucker blinked in disbelief. "Wait a minute! Pizza?! In . . . PRISON?!!"

I was like, DUH! You go to PRISON for burglary!

"What is it, Einstein?!" Ralph taunted. "Having second thoughts?"

"I'm just thinking. If there's pizza in prison, I could order Mighty Meat Monster. Or maybe sausage with pepperoni and green peppers. Last week I had ham with pineapple and mushrooms. That was delish!"

"And prison food is free, right? Can you imagine hot, cheesy FREE pizza?!" Moose drooled.

Ralph shook his head in complete disgust. Then he closed his eyes and rubbed his temples.

"Both of you . . . just stop talking, okay? STOP! TALKING!" he growled as his face turned beet red. "THE NEXT PERSON WHO OPENS HIS BIG MOUTH IS GONNA GET SOMETHING TO EAT! A KNUCKLE SANDWICH! GOT THAT?!!"

Moose and Tucker frantically nodded, their mouths shut so tightly, it looked like they'd been sucking on tubes of superglue. It was so quiet, you could hear a pin drop. Then suddenly . . .

BEEP-BEEP!

BEEP-BEEP!

BEEP-BEEP! . . .

The three men froze as their eyes darted nervously around the room—they clearly were afraid they'd somehow set off a burglar alarm.

Actually, the burglar alarm sounded really familiar. And, weirder yet, it seemed to be coming from very close by.

I looked down at my wrist and gulped.

OH, CRUD!!

I couldn't believe this was actually happening to me. That's when I very awkwardly muttered . . .

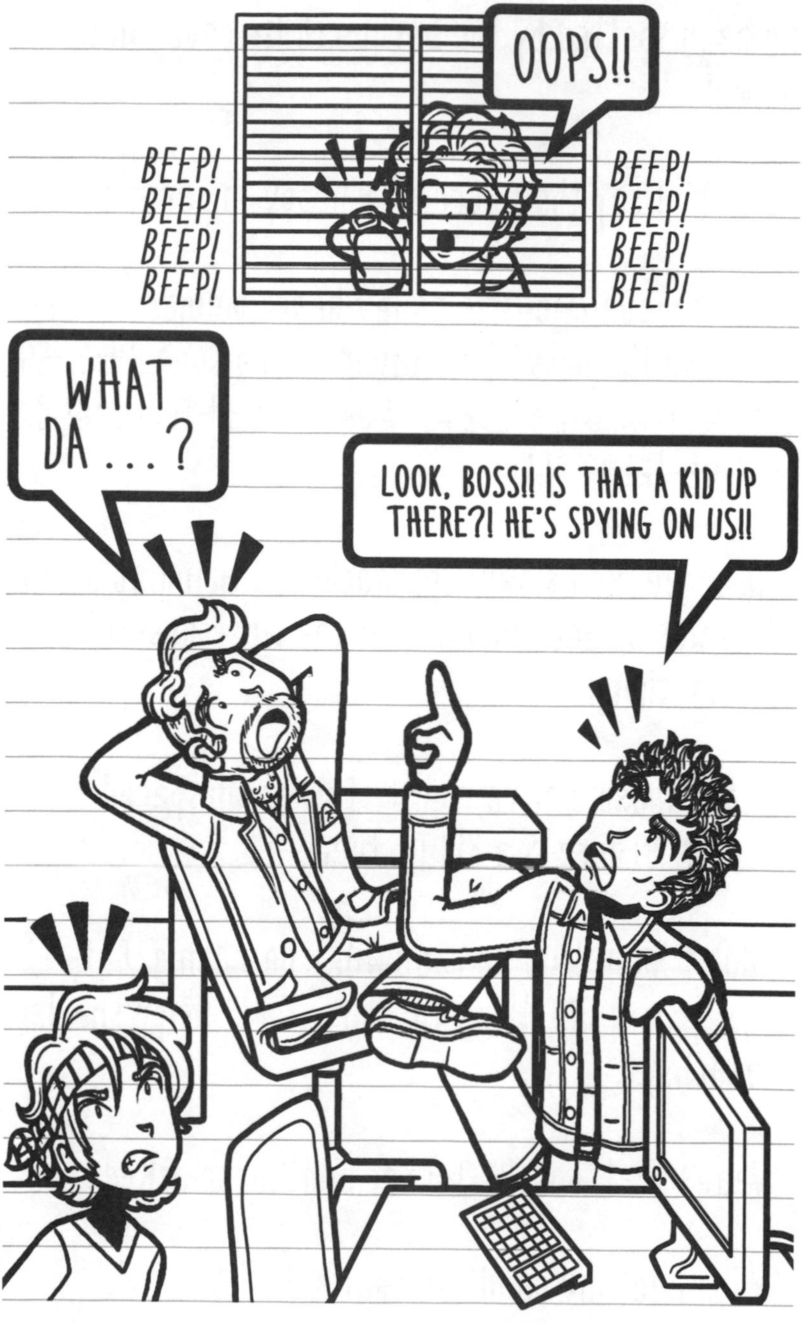
BEEP!
BEEP!
BEEP!
BEEP!
OOPS!!
BEEP!
BEEP!
BEEP!
BEEP!
WHAT DA . . . ?
LOOK, BOSS!! IS THAT A KID UP THERE?! HE'S SPYING ON US!!

I'd been spotted by the burglars!! My cover was blown!

Let's just say they were NOT happy to see me.

I didn't move a muscle as my heart pounded in my ears like the bass in my favorite rap song. ~~I was SO scared, I almost pooped my pants right there inside that vent! FOR REAL!~~

The three men slowly approached, staring up at me like I was a caged monkey at the Westchester Zoo or something!

"Yeah, Moose, you're right!" Tucker whispered gruffly. "There IS a kid up there!"

"I don't know WHO he is or WHAT he's doing. But, guys, I know ONE thing for sure . . . !" Ralph snarled menacingly.

"What's that, boss?" Tucker and Moose asked.

"When I get my hands on that kid . . ."

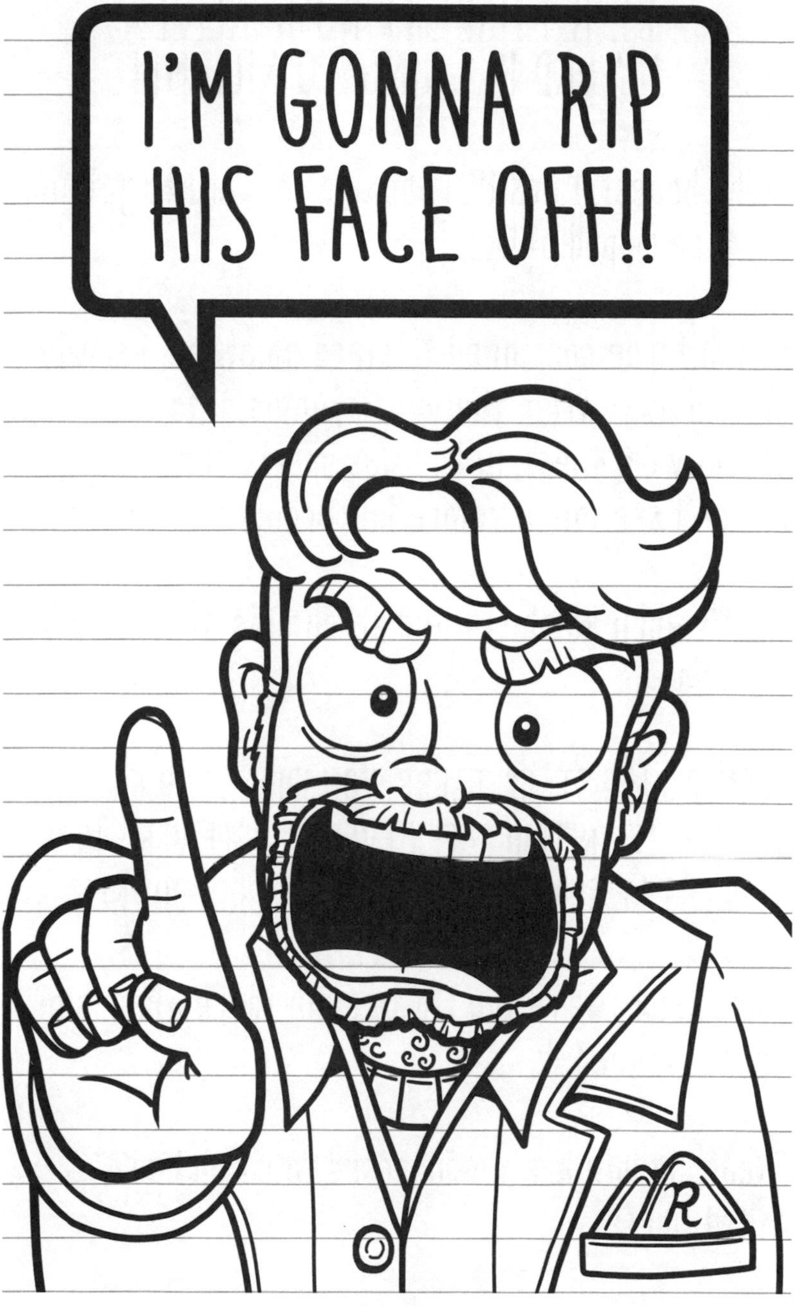
I'M GONNA RIP HIS FACE OFF!!

21. IF I MAKE IT HOME ALIVE, MY DAD IS GOING TO KILL ME!

To be honest, I was NOT looking forward to getting my face ripped off.

As the three continued to stare up at me, I slowly backed away from the vent opening, into the shadowy darkness, until I was pretty sure they couldn't see me anymore but I could still see them.

That's when Ralph started screaming at the top of his lungs. . . .

"DON'T JUST STAND THERE, YOU IDIOTS!! GO CATCH THE LITTLE SNITCH! CHECK EVERY SINGLE VENT IN THIS ENTIRE SCHOOL UNTIL WE HUNT HIM DOWN!"

"But, Ralph, we're too big to go in there after him," Tucker argued.

"Yeah, so how are we supposed to catch him?" asked Moose.

"Just FIND him, you MEATHEADS, and leave the rest to me!" Ralph growled.

"Okay, Ralph. But can we at least take a little break for dinner first?" Tucker asked.

"You want a BREAK?! I'll give you a break! I'LL BREAK YOUR NOSE!" Ralph hollered as he picked up a magazine from a nearby desk and rolled it into a weapon. "HERE'S your stinking BREAK!"

WHACK! He smacked Tucker upside his head!

"OUCH!" Tucker yelled.

"I told both of you to EAT before we left, but NO! You NEVER listen!"

WHACK! He smacked Moose upside his head.

"OW!" Moose bellowed.

"Still hungry? Here's some DESSERT!"

WHACK! He smacked Tucker again.

"HEY!" Tucker said, staring up at the magazine. "Dude, just hold up for a second! Let me take a closer look at that mag, okay?"

"How about I just shove it down your throat for wasting my valuable time? Will that be CLOSE enough for you?" Ralph grumbled.

"Sheesh, Ralph! Just chillax, will you?" Tucker snatched the magazine out of his boss's hand and squinted at the small print on the front cover.

"This ain't the library. Read on your OWN time, you IDIOT!" Ralph spat.

"NO WAY! This looks like a limited-edition *COMICS DIGEST* from 1972. I'm pretty sure it's worth BIG BUCKS!" Tucker exclaimed.

My heart skipped a beat! It sounded like he was describing my dad's comic book! I inched forward to take a closer look!

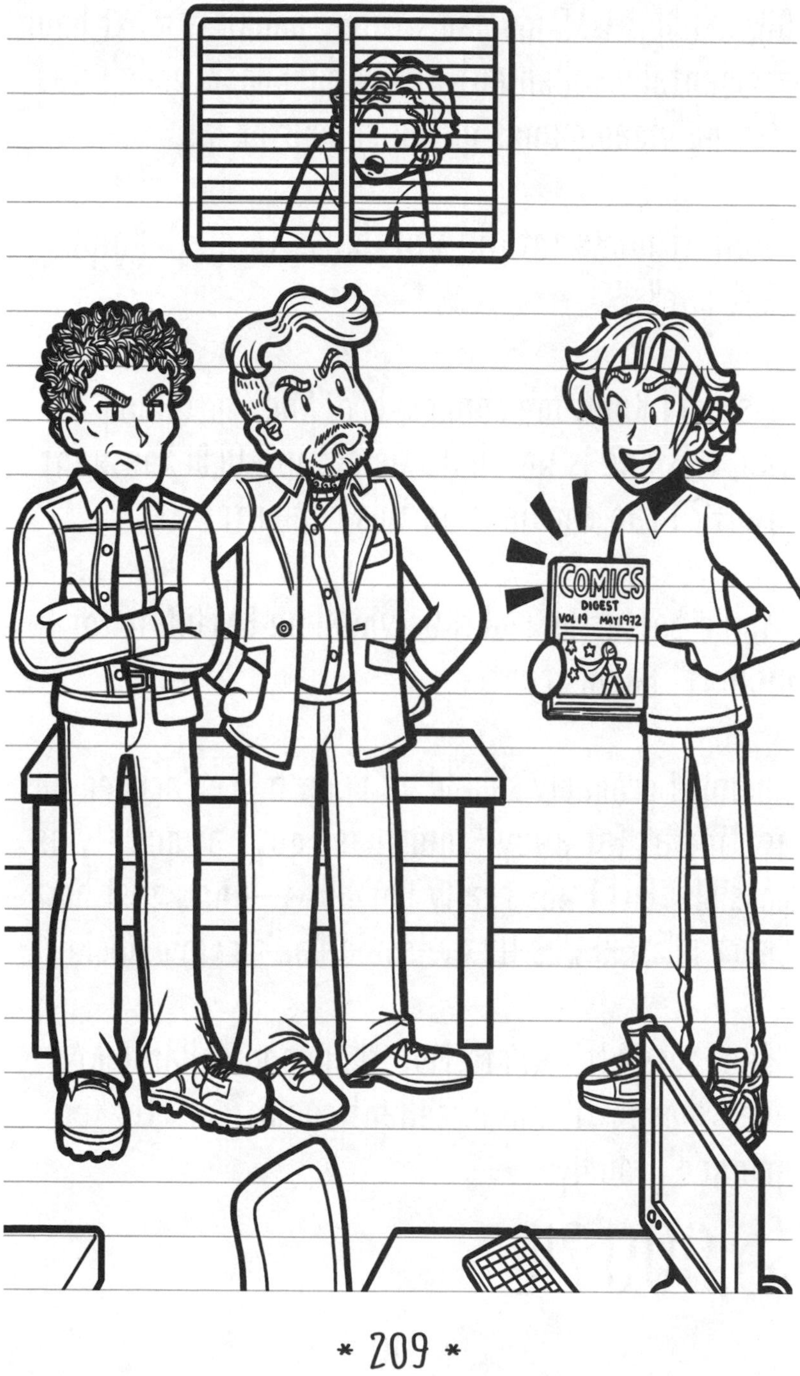
COMICS
DIGEST
VOL 19 MAY 1972

OH, CRUD! It WAS my dad's comic book!! It must have accidentally fallen out of my backpack while I was playing video games in the computer lab.

"Well, it looks totally worthless to me!" Ralph shot back.

"Listen! I know my comics, bro. And I'm telling you, this one is worth its weight in GOLD! You want proof? I can google it on this computer."

"You'd better be right! Or you'll be EATING it for dinner!" Ralph grunted.

I admit I probably should've been more focused on getting as far away from those guys as quickly as possible. But I was really curious ~~to know just how BADLY I'd SCREWED UP by losing Dad's comic book~~!

"See, boss? It's worth five thousand dollars!! And even more if it's in excellent condition!" Tucker grinned proudly.

$5,000?!!!

I felt like I had just gotten sucker punched in my gut!

"BOO-YAH! There's nothing like easy money, boys!" Ralph exclaimed. "Tucker, why didn't you say something before I smacked you with it? I could have damaged this VERY valuable comic book on your CONCRETE HEAD. Now hand it over!"

"Wait a minute!" Tucker protested. "You said we'd get a cut of ALL the merchandise. And that includes this comic book! So for now let's just leave it right here on this table for safekeeping."

Just great! Those thugs were stealing the school's computers AND my dad's $5,000 comic book!!

I turned around and started crawling back through the vents as fast as my arms and legs could carry me!

I went fifty-five yards and made a right turn, and then I went another thirty yards and made a left.

I ended up in a long corridor with no vent openings. It was the perfect place to stop and rest.

All I could hear were the faint muffled voices of the men still arguing about the comic book, and my heart pounding in my chest like a bass drum.

Beads of sweat dripped off my forehead, and my hands and knees were stinging from the friction of crawling.

I sat up, hugged my knees, and closed my eyes. I was starting to feel really light-headed. That's when I suddenly realized I was holding my breath.

Okay, Crumbly! Get a grip! NOT breathing will make it kind of difficult to stay alive. I took two large whiffs from my inhaler and tried to breathe deeply.

The only thing WORSE than being locked in the school alone after hours?

Being locked in the school after hours with three RUTHLESS burglars! All intent on ripping my face off!

This was some serious stuff!

Where were the hall monitors when you REALLY needed them?!

Somebody had to stop those crooks. But, unfortunately, I was the only "somebody" around.

My gut told me to step up and be a hero. But my lungs were like, "No way! There are three of them against one of you. So let's just go hide out in our safe and cozy locker until these criminals pack up and leave!"

Um, okay. I'll admit my lungs had a valid point.

Yes, I was a totally useless coward. And I didn't have six-pack abs like Thug Thurston.

But I DID have BRAINS and my trusty inhaler. I'd made it to level forty-nine in the Valiant Knights of the Galaxy video game in only three days.

And I was pretty much an expert on superheroes and villains from reading hundreds of comic books.

But, most importantly, I needed to try to get my dad's comic back ~~before he realized it was missing and strangled me~~!

That's when I came up with a BRILLIANT plan.

While those men were busy loading up the computers, I'd simply crawl through the vents to the school office, grab a phone, and dial 911! Then I'd sneak back to the computer lab and swipe Dad's comic book in the ten minutes it would take the police to arrive, and *BAM!!* I'd be an instant HERO and a local CELEBRITY!

SWEET!

Then if Thug wanted to try to start something with me again, he'd have a HUGE fight on his hands.

Why?

Because he'd have to FIGHT his way through my very large throng of friends, admirers, autograph seekers, and cute girls who were crushing on me!

My life would NEVER be the same. I couldn't help smiling at the thought of it all. . . .

ME

I mentally mapped out my trip to the office. Estimated time of arrival: 2.5 minutes. However, just as I was about to crawl past a vent in the main hall, I ran into a slight complication.

Well, actually THREE slight complications! RALPH, TUCKER, and MOOSE! I hung back a few feet so they couldn't see me.

"Okay, so this is the plan. I'll take the north wing. Tucker, you take the west wing, and Moose, you take the east wing. Now move it! We gotta find that kid before it's too late!" Ralph scowled. Then he strode quickly down the hall and disappeared.

"This school is HUGE! We're never gonna find that kid!" Tucker complained. "We should just grab the computers and get outta here while we can, but Ralph is so stubborn, he won't listen!"

"Forget Ralph! I've got an even BETTER idea!" Moose said, and winked.

"DUDE!! Are YOU thinking what I'M thinking?" Tucker snickered.

"Yeah, BRO! It'll be just YOU and ME!" Moose chuckled.

"Awesome!" Tucker exclaimed.

"Let's roll! We gotta be done before Ralph comes back!" Moose said as he took off running.

"Hey, Moose! Wait up!" Tucker yelled as he scampered off after him.

I didn't have the slightest idea what those two were up to. Although it sounded to me like they were planning to double-cross Ralph. But as long as they stayed out of MY way, I didn't care. I scurried through the vents, and within minutes I'd reached my final destination. . . .

THE MAIN OFFICE!! That's when I noticed all the lights in the school had been turned on by the burglars.

I popped open the vent and quickly lowered myself to the floor. Then I dashed to the phone, grabbed it, and dialed 911. I glanced cautiously over my shoulder and then whispered loudly. . . .

HELLO! THIS IS AN EMERGENCY! I WANT TO REPORT A BURGLARY IN PROGRESS AT SOUTH RIDGE MIDDLE SCHOOL!!

22. HOW "CINDERELLA" LOST
A ~~GLASS SLIPPER~~ SNEAKER

"Excuse me! But WHAT are you talking about?!" said a highly annoyed teen girl on the other end of the line. "Is this a prank phone call or something?"

"NO! This ISN'T a prank call! It's an EMERGENCY! Um, is this 911?" I asked, confused.

"Sorry, but this is Queasy Cheesy! If you're trying to call 911, you dialed the wrong number! Good-bye!"

"WAIT!! Don't hang up! We're just TRYIN' to order a pizza! With cheesy breadsticks!" said a very familiar voice. "I got a thirty-percent-off coupon."

"Don't forget the buffalo wings!" a voice in the background chimed in.

"Right! And buffalo wings, too!"

It was Tucker and Moose! I couldn't believe they were actually ordering a pizza, cheesy breadsticks, and wings while burglarizing the school!

"I'll leave the money in an envelope at the front door of South Ridge Middle School, and you can just leave my order, okay? We're working here late tonight. Now, did you get all of that? I don't want you getting confused and screwing up my order," Moose said.

"Excuse me, but YOU'RE the one who's totally CONFUSED! Do you want to order pizza, or do you have an emergency? You really need to make up your mind! I'm supposed to be on break right now," the girl on the phone explained impatiently.

"Who said anything about an emergency?" Moose asked, starting to get irritated.

I tried to deepen my voice. "Yo! This is . . . ME, um . . . the pizza delivery GUY! And I have an emergency! I'm out of pizza . . . um, delivery . . . boxes?!"

"Oh, really! So THIS must be Michael, right? My BFF, Emily, said you broke up with her at lunch today for no reason!" the girl said angrily.

"Actually, I'm NOT Michael! I'm the . . . um, OTHER pizza delivery guy, okay?" I lied.

"Don't LIE to me, Michael! You might lie to Emily, but don't even try that with ME."

"Listen, lady! How long will it take before you'll be delivering our order? We're STARVING!" Moose whined.

"Um, can I please speak to the manager, then?" I pleaded. "About my, um . . . pizza box situation?"

"You don't NEED to talk to the manager right now, Michael! You NEED to be talking to EMILY!"

"But I'm NOT Michael! And I DON'T want to talk to Emily!"

"Are we going to get that free order of extra-spicy wings like the TV commercial says?!" Tucker asked.

"You know what, Michael? Just forget it! Emily is SO over you!"

CLICK!! (That's when the phone went dead!)

Suddenly I heard a loud tapping sound!! And when I turned around . . .

I TOTALLY FREAKED!!

It was MOOSE and TUCKER!

They were in the principal's office right behind me!

I ran, jumped, and pulled my body up into the front of the ventilation tunnel all in one motion . . .

Just as Tucker and Moose burst into the room!

They looked a bit confused when it appeared that I had disappeared into thin air.

Finally Moose looked up. "LOOK!!" he said, pointing. "The kid is escaping into that VENT!!"

"You're NOT going to get away THIS time, you little . . . !!" Tucker yelled as he dove across the room and grabbed my foot.

"GOTCHA!!" Moose shouted as he held on to my leg with a vise-like grip.

Then they both started to pull me out of the vent.

I tried to hold on with all my strength, but it was no use.

I was no match for the two of them. . . .

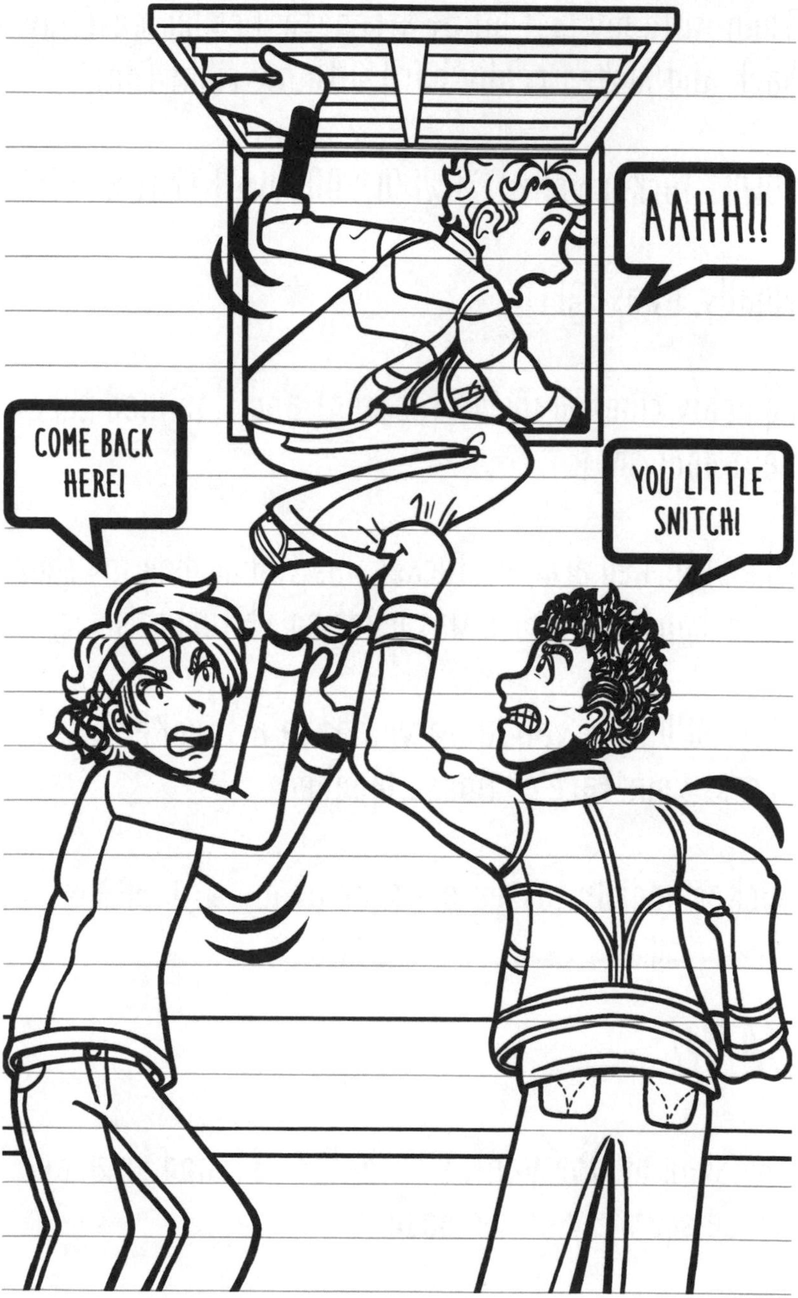
AAHH!!
COME BACK HERE!
YOU LITTLE SNITCH!

Then, with my last bit of strength, I rolled onto my back and kicked really hard with my right foot.

"OW!!" Tucker yelled. "OW! OW! OOOOWW! That HURT!!"

Finally, I was FREE!!

I quickly climbed inside the vent and slammed the vent door shut.

When I turned around, Tucker was still holding my shoe in his hand and Moose was pointing at Tucker's face.

"Um, DUDE! Did you know you have a sneaker print across your face?" Moose laughed.

Tucker angrily tossed my shoe at me with all his strength!!

BAM!!

The shoe hit the vent, ricocheted off, and smacked Moose squarely on his nose.

"OOOOOUCH!!" he howled in pain. "What'd you do dat for, Tucker? I tink you boke by nose!!"

"What's wrong, bro?! You're NOT laughing anymore?! Dude, did you know you have a sneaker print across your nose?!" Tucker snorted.

Both men turned and glared at me.

Moose picked up my shoe and slowly waved it back and forth in front of the vent as he spoke in a high-pitched, squeaky voice, just to mock me.

"Come back, Cinderella! You lost your shoe! Don't you want your beautiful little shoe? Come back, Cinderella!"

Then they both doubled over in laughter.

I just rolled my eyes at them.

HA-HA! Very FUNNY, I thought. Almost as funny as my sneaker prints embedded on your faces.

Safely back inside the vent system, I crawled twenty yards, hung a quick right, and crawled thirty-five yards.

My 911 call had been hijacked.

I'd almost gotten caught by the burglars.

I was missing a shoe.

And I'd been called Cinderella.

My Plan A had failed horribly.

So now it was time for Plan B.

Unfortunately, I didn't have one!

23. ATTACK OF THE KILLER TOILET!

I wanted to get as far away from those crooks as possible.

And FAST!!

After that fiasco in the office, the three of them had launched a massive MANHUNT for me.

They were checking the vents in the main hallway with flashlights. So trying to avoid getting caught by them was going to become even MORE difficult.

Suddenly I remembered the LAST place I'd want to be in this ENTIRE school.

The boys' bathroom on the south end!

My school is really old and has had a lot of major renovation work. But they were too cheap to fix up that bathroom, so it has cobwebs and is hardly ever cleaned.

And since most of the toilets are out of order or don't flush properly, it smells like a sewer.

However, here's the WEIRDEST part about that bathroom!! . . .

A guy from my PE class, named Cody Locks, claims a wild raccoon family lives in there.

Yeah, I know! It sounds pretty ridiculous to ME, too.

Hey, I'm not sure if raccoons are dangerous or not. But no guy from our school was willing to take a chance on being ~~caught with his pants down when that raccoon family unexpectedly returned home from a walk in the woods and found him~~ in there!

Practically EVERYONE had heard the famous SCHOOL LEGEND about . . .

CODY LOCKS AND

THE THREE ~~BEARS~~ RACCOONS

CODY MEETS THE RACCOON FAMILY!

So yeah! Being viciously attacked by an unfriendly family of raccoons was a risk I was willing to take.

When I finally arrived at that bathroom, it was in even worse shape than I remembered. Instead of water in the toilets, there was a thick, black muck the consistency of mud.

BARF!!

An Out of Order sign was taped on the wall, and some kid had scribbled the word "VERY" across the top and doodled a sad face at the bottom.

I wondered if his graffiti message was some kind of cryptic WARNING.

Unfortunately, as I was climbing down from the vent, my foot slipped and I accidentally flushed the toilet.

Let's just say what happened next ~~left me severely emotionally SCARRED for the rest of my LIFE!!~~ was totally UNEXPECTED!! . . .

I ACCIDENTALLY FLUSHED THE TOILET!

I GOT SPRAYED WITH STINKY MUCK!

THEN I FELL INTO THE STINKY MUCK!!

I REALLY **HATE** CRYPTIC WARNINGS 😦!

I smelled WORSE than ~~a bucket of two-day-old cow poop steaming in the hot sun in the middle of July!~~ anything I'd ever smelled in my entire life!

And that was just WRONG on so many levels!

Anyway, there was good news and bad news.

The good news was that, despite the school legend, I was NOT attacked by a pack of rabid raccoons while I was in that bathroom.

The bad news was that I needed to find a change of clothing ASAP!!

Before the horrific stench of the muck completely KILLED OFF the few remaining healthy BRAIN CELLS I had left!

24. OUT OF LUCK, COVERED IN MUCK, AND DRENCHED IN STENCH

I quickly decided that traveling through the vents was going to be too dangerous. Once the burglars got a good whiff of me, they would be able to track me down anywhere in the entire school just by the smell alone.

And if they found me, I'd be DEAD MEAT!!

~~Which would be a really BIG coincidence since I already SMELLED like rotting DEAD MEAT!!~~

I snuck out of the bathroom and ~~quietly~~ tiptoed down the hallway. . . .

SQUIRK! SQUIRK! SQUIRK! SQUIRK!

Every step I took made an annoying sound and left a very smelly trail of black muck behind me. I barely had time to duck behind a large plant when I spotted the burglars coming out of the school office in an adjoining hall.

Ralph was talking on his cell phone, but his face was pale and he looked like he'd just seen a ghost!

"Calm down, Tina!! Please, dear! I'm sorry! I completely forgot your mother was coming for dinner!" he sputtered nervously. "No! I wasn't trying to disrespect her! Listen, I'll wrap up this business meeting and be home soon, okay? . . . Yeah, I love you, too, sweetheart! Bye."

Ralph took out his hankie and wiped the sweat off his face. "I HATE it when Tina interrupts me when I'm trying to work!!" he grumbled.

"Your wife is EVIL, man!" Tucker laughed. "She's even SCARIER than you are!"

"Who's the big BABY now, huh?!" Moose snickered. "Ralph, you were SO scared, it smells like you just POOPED your pants!"

I couldn't help rolling my eyes! Actually, that SMELL was, um . . . ME!! I desperately fanned the air, trying to dissipate the foul odor.

"Just SHUT UP already, you NUMBSKULLS!!" Ralph barked. "I cut the phone lines, but we still need to find that kid! He's the only person who can identify us. We haven't searched the south wing yet. So, you two, get on it!"

THE SOUTH WING?!! I gasped! That meant Tucker and Moose were headed in my direction.

I took off running! *SQUIRK! SQUIRK! SQUIRK!*

I tried the boys' locker room, but the door was locked. DANG!! So I dashed across the hall and cautiously peeked around a corner as my heart pounded in my chest!

"Hey, Tucker! Did you hear that squeaking noise?! It might be the kid! Follow me!" Moose exclaimed as they both sped toward the sound.

I held my breath as Moose and Tucker came barreling down another hall in my direction.

They were less than twenty feet away when I heard . . .

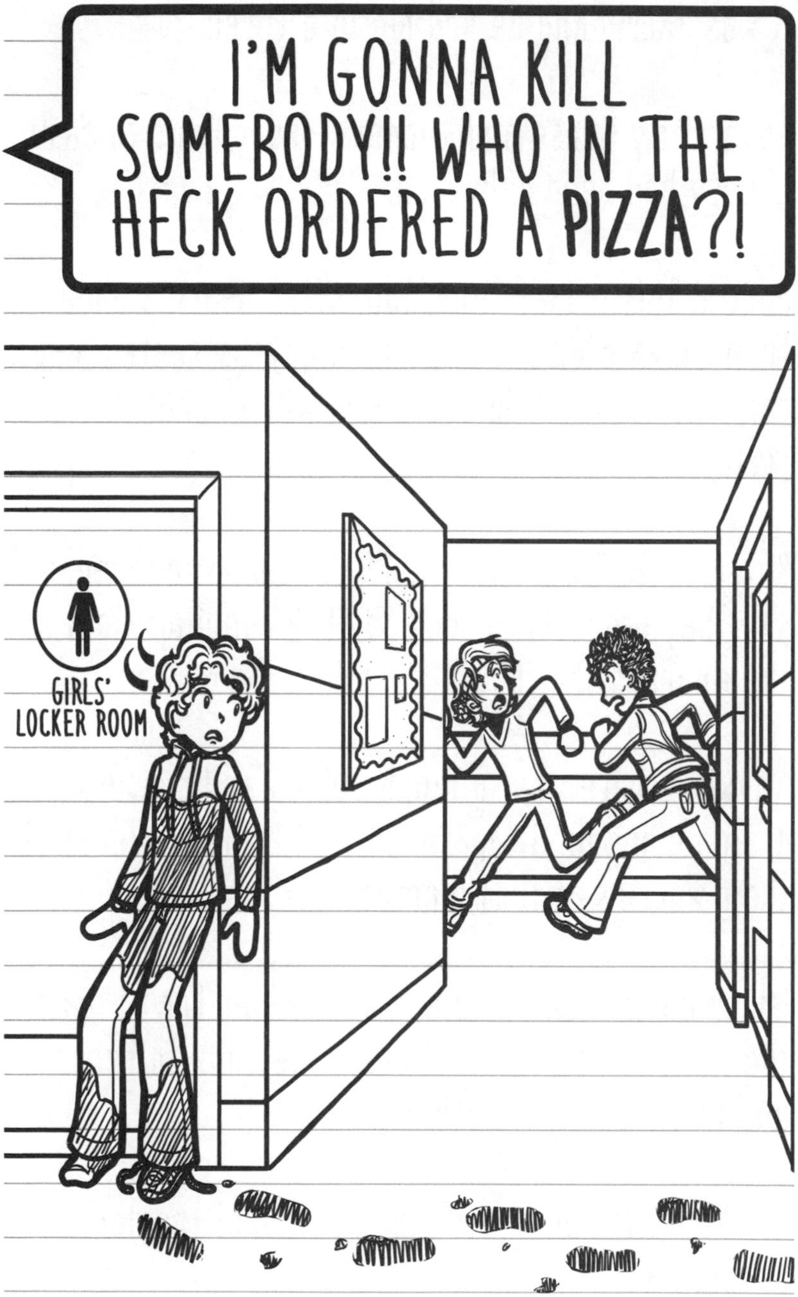

I'M GONNA KILL SOMEBODY!! WHO IN THE HECK ORDERED A PIZZA?!
GIRLS' LOCKER ROOM

It was RALPH! And he had blown a fuse!!

Apparently Moose and Tucker's order from Queasy Cheesy had been delivered.

Just in the nick of time, too. After hearing about their pizza order, the two men got distracted and ran right past my hiding place! WHEW! That was a close call!

But judging from how TICKED OFF Ralph sounded, I'd say they probably needed to KEEP running! Right out the nearest EXIT DOOR!

Anyway, there was so much ~~yelling and cursing~~ drama going on, it appeared that I was the least of their worries at that moment.

Which meant they'd be out of my hair for at least the next ten minutes and give me time to regroup and come up with another plan.

I sighed with relief and leaned against the door behind me.

Surprisingly, it was unlocked and swung open.

So I decided to go inside. . . .

Yes, I know. I KNOW!! You're probably thinking . . .

DUDE, YOU'VE LOST YOUR MIND!!

YOU'RE GOING INSIDE THE GIRLS' LOCKER ROOM?!!

THAT'S JUST WRONG ON SO MANY LEVELS!!

Sorry! But ~~I was finally going to be able to use the bathroom, thank goodness!~~ I was so EXHAUSTED, so DESPERATE, and so SCARED . . .

I didn't even care!

25. WHY THERE WAS A BOY IN THE GIRLS' LOCKER ROOM

Listen up, people! I really have to get this off my chest.

Only an extremely IMMATURE person would make a big deal out of a guy going into the girls' locker room.

Don't get it TWISTED! It was an EMERGENCY! And I only had TWO options:

1. Run around the school ~~NAKED~~ in my birthday suit, or

2. Search for clothes in the forbidden realm known as the GIRLS' LOCKER ROOM.

Like I said earlier, I DIDN'T EVEN CARE!

Well, I have a confession to make. . . .

I LIED!!

Once I actually stepped INSIDE the girls' locker room, I totally FREAKED OUT!

For some reason, I started shivering like crazy.

I wasn't sure if it was the cold draft from the air conditioner or if I was just completely PETRIFIED of facing the GIRLY UNKNOWN.

"Get a grip, Crumbly!" I mumbled to myself. "This is a LIFE-or-DEATH situation!"

But I wasn't talking about Tucker, Moose, and Ralph.

If I didn't get out of my muck-covered clothes soon, the STINK was going to KILL me BEFORE those guys ever caught up with me!

I grabbed my inhaler and took several deep breaths (while holding my nose).

Then I decided to look around.

Well, the good news is that I learned something new.

The girls' locker room looks a lot like the boys' locker room.

I guess I expected a pink palace filled with rainbows, cupcakes, and baby unicorns!

Hey, what do I know about girls?!

I searched through most of the lockers, and they were empty.

Not a single piece of clothing ANYWHERE!

That's when I started to panic.

Come on! HOW could this be happening?!

Wasn't this a GIRLS' LOCKER ROOM, for crying out loud?!!

I was about to give up hope ~~and burst into tears~~.

But, luckily, I hit the jackpot with one of the lockers on the back wall. . . .

FINALLY I FOUND SOME CLOTHES!

AWESOME! I couldn't wait to get out of my filthy "Poopy Couture" rags!

I planned to toss them right where they belonged. In the TOILET!

Sorry, Mr. Janitor! Just call it poetic justice.

I took a closer look at the outfit and instantly realized I had a bit of a fashion crisis on my hands.

~~Why did girls' clothing have to be so, um . . . GIRLY?!~~

It was a shimmery baby-blue one-piece bodysuit thing, with a sewn-on silver metallic cape and a tacky mom belt!

The ultra-stretchy, shiny leotard fabric looked like it could easily expand to fit me ~~and three members of the soccer team~~.

A sheer skirt decorated with sequins and sparkly snowflakes was neatly folded on the top shelf, and I planned to leave it right there.

Sorry, but that outfit was a HOT MESS! All I needed was a glittery pink BLINDFOLD to complete the look, and then I wouldn't have to actually SEE myself.

I also noticed that the shoe bag was monogrammed with the letter *E*.

I know quite a few females whose names begin with that letter, like Erma, Edna, and Ethel.

Obviously, their names AREN'T as POPULAR for teens as the name Erin, but I was homeschooled, remember?

And Erma, Edna, and Ethel are nice, elderly ladies who hung out at my grandma's house and played bingo on Saturdays at the senior center.

~~Did I mention that Ethel makes REALLY GOOD snickerdoodle cookies?~~

Anyway, I spotted a crumpled packet of papers on the floor of the locker. It was a script for the play *The Ice Princess* and a cast list. And the only person in the cast whose name started with *E* was Erin!

So there was no doubt about it! I was RAIDING Erin Madison's PE locker!! NOOOO!!

That totally made me a SICKO, right?! I turned red with embarrassment and slammed her locker shut.

Sure, I felt like a total CREEP borrowing ~~my crush's~~ another student's clothing.

But I HAD to get rid of my cold, wet, stinky, sewage-covered clothing because it was probably a BIOHAZARD!

~~What if I was carrying bacteria in my shirt pocket more deadly than the BUBONIC PLAGUE?! I could accidentally KILL OFF all of HUMANKIND!~~

So, ~~in my heroic attempt to save the world,~~ I made the decision to borrow Erin's *Ice Princess* costume.

If I took it to the dry cleaner and placed it back inside the locker after I'd worn it, she'd never even know it was missing.

Next I needed to find some shoes.

Although my new nickname is Cinderella, I was NOT feeling that three-inch-tall, fake-diamond-encrusted, princessy, um, footwear. . . .

CUTE, YES! BUT NOT QUITE ME.

I had better luck scavenging in the lost-and-found box.

I snagged a cool pair of leather boots with buckles, perfect for riding a fast and furious motorcycle. . . .

But that wasn't even the BEST part!

I also found a CELL PHONE! And it actually worked! SWEET!

I decided to borrow it temporarily, just in case something went down and I REALLY needed to use it. Having a phone made me feel like a huge weight had been lifted off my shoulders—once I got the comic book back, I could use it to call the police.

I quickly changed and tried not to think about the fact that I was wearing Erin's clothing. Even though I knew I was going to look silly, I couldn't resist checking myself out in a nearby full-length mirror.

"WHOA!!" I muttered to myself as I blinked in surprise.

Yeah, I'd probably get laughed at or punched in the face at school.

But I'd get mad props and a dozen fist bumps at COMIC-CON! . . .

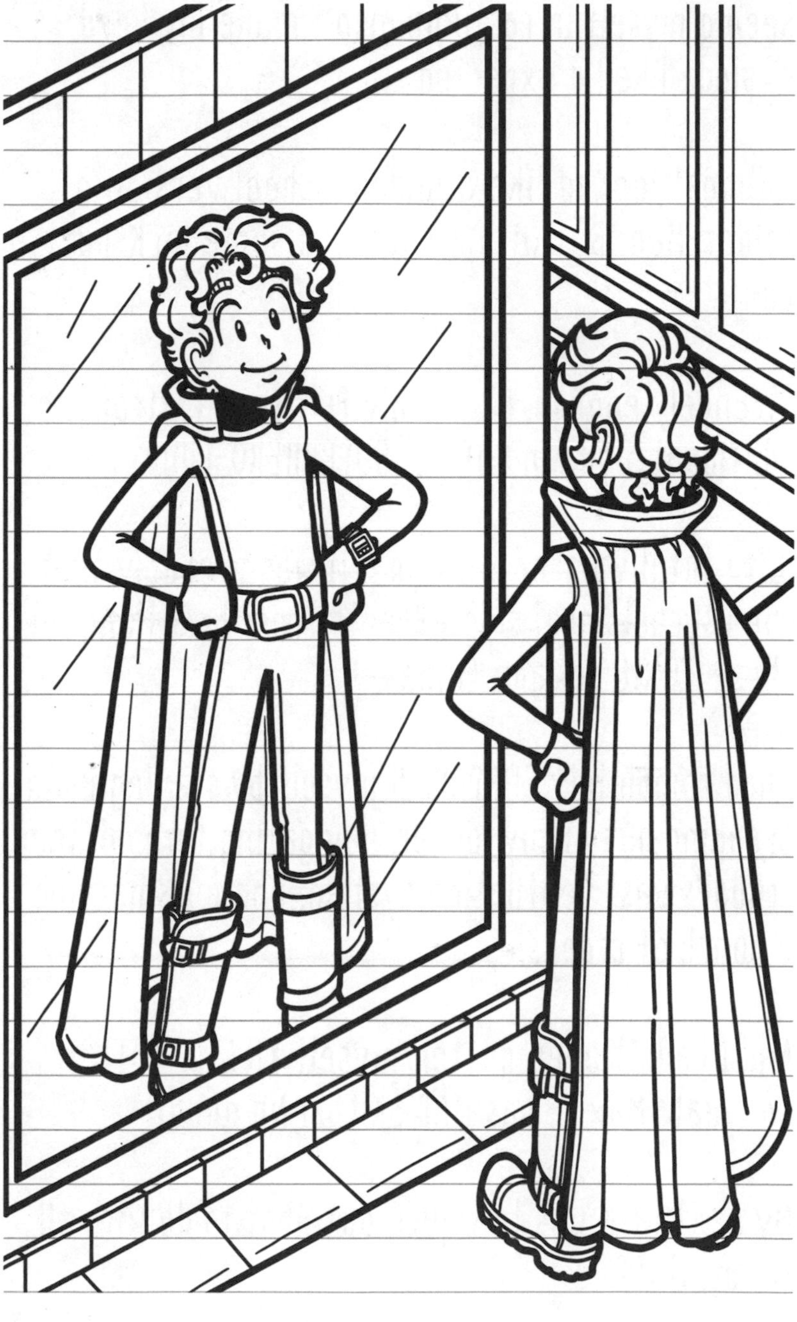

Seeing myself in costume didn't make my head explode like I'd expected.

I almost looked like a middle school version of Spider-Man. But with a cape and some kick-butt boots.

Strangely enough, I suddenly felt smart, strong, confident, and kind of . . . SUPERHERO-ISH!

~~But I totally agree with you. It was probably just the psychological side effects from breathing all those TOXIC sewage fumes.~~

I had completely SURPRISED myself by staying calm, breaking out of my locker, navigating through the school's vast ventilation system, and outsmarting a bunch of crooks.

And I hadn't even gotten myself KILLED. YET!
So, yeah. Max C. has MAD SKILLZ! No doubt!

My next task was to figure out what to do with all of my stuff.

The costume had a back pocket that was supposed to hold a microphone receiver.

It was a tight fit, but I managed to stuff my journal and inhaler and the cell phone inside.

Since there wasn't room for my flashlight, I bent over and shoved it into the top of my boot.

FINALLY! I was ready to begin my QUEST to retrieve my dad's comic book and stop the burglars from stealing the school's computers.

But there was one thing that I WASN'T quite ready for: a strange voice from behind me that said . . .

"HELLO?!"

26. WORST. RINGTONE. EVER!!

As far as I knew, the ONLY other people in the building were Tucker, Moose, and Ralph. So I totally expected to hear MALE voices yelling and talking SMACK about ripping my face off! But this was a GIRL'S voice!

"HELLO?!" she said again.

I froze and nervously glanced around the room.

"Who s-said that?! Who's th-there?!" I stammered.

The only thing I saw out of place was a large dead roach. I shuddered. EWW!! Ever since my grandma's new neighbors moved in a few weeks ago, it's like I've developed a phobia of roaches. It's probably because the dad drives a creepy van that has a humongous roach on top of it.

~~And whenever I walked past the thing, I half-expected it to snatch me up and bite my head off like an evil praying mantis or something. Hey, don't laugh! Dude, I've had some really SCARY nightmares!~~

But bugs can't talk. Especially DEAD ones.

Then the girl's voice spoke again. "HELLO?! WHO is this?!"

That's when I noticed the voice was close. VERY close! Like right BEHIND me. I spun around in a panic, but no one was there. Okay, this was INSANE! Was the girls' locker room haunted? Or had my WORST fear come true?

"OH NO!" I shrieked hysterically. "I'm hearing voices! Those TOXIC sewage fumes have killed off the few brain cells I had left! And now I'm irreversibly brain damaged!"

"Really?! Well, that's a pretty LAME excuse for stealing my cell phone and then prank-calling me," the girl answered sarcastically. "But you obviously have some issues."

That's when I realized the voice WASN'T coming from inside my head. It was actually coming from . . .

MY BUTT?!

I quickly grabbed the cell phone out of my back pocket and stared at it. Then she said . . .

"Um . . . HELLO?! I'm REALLY sorry about all of this! I didn't mean to call you. It was an accident. Honest!" I apologized profusely. "GOOD-BYE!"

Then I clicked the red button to end the call.

Problem solved.

"HEY, BOSS! COME LOOK AT THESE MUDDY FOOTPRINTS!
I BET THEY'RE FROM THAT KID!" someone shouted
from down the hall.

It was TUCKER! The burglars were HOT on my trail
AGAIN!

Suddenly the cell phone started blasting a cheesy
boy band song! . . .

"LISTEN, GURL! WE HAVE A CONNECTION! I LUV U MORE
THAN MY LEGO COLLECTION!"

I cringed. WORST. RINGTONE. EVER!

Most girls, including my sister, Megan, have
been playing that boy band song NONSTOP since
it came out a few weeks ago. I absolutely HATE
it! ~~I could eat a bowl of alphabet soup and POOP~~
~~better lyrics!~~

But please don't tell my PSYCHO-FAN sister I said that! ~~She'd crush my skull like an empty juice box!~~

I quickly answered the phone, mostly just to stop that crappy song from playing. "HELLO?!"

"I CAN'T believe you just HUNG UP on me!" the girl said icily.

"Listen, I can't talk right now!" I said, starting to get annoyed. "I'm really busy, okay?"

"Let me guess! You're busy stealing more cell phones?!" she shot back.

"I didn't STEAL your phone! WHO is this?"

"What do you mean, 'WHO is this?' Who are YOU?" she snapped. "You've got A LOT of nerve, prank-calling my home phone number!"

"I didn't do it on purpose. I must have accidentally BUTT-DIALED you. I found your phone in the lost-and-found box in the girls' locker room. I'm just borrowing it, okay? And after I'm done using it, I'll put it right back in there. I promise! Good-bye!"

CLICK! I hung up on her again. Problem solved!

"SOME OF THESE FOOTPRINTS LEAD TO THE BOYS' LOCKER ROOM!! I BET HE'S STILL IN THERE!" Moose yelled.

Now they were right across the hall. I rushed to lock MY door, but it required a key. OH, CRUD!!

The phone started blasting that stupid song again. . . .

"LISTEN, GURL! WE HAVE A CONNECTION! I LUV U MORE THAN MY LEGO COLLECTION!"

I glanced nervously at the door, hoping the crooks didn't hear the music, and quickly answered the phone. "HELLO? I'm sorry you lost your phone. But you really need to STOP CALLING me, okay?"

"WHAT were you doing in the GIRLS' LOCKER ROOM?!" the girl yelled. "On second thought, I don't even want to know the answer!"

"It's not what you think! I just needed some clean . . . Forget it. Listen, I'm going to hang up now. But PLEASE don't call me again. You're going to get me KILLED!" I whisper-shouted. "It's kind of an emergency. I'm dealing with some deranged burglars! And I don't want them to hear your phone ringing!"

"BURGLARS?!! Seriously?!" the girl exclaimed. "You should have told me that to begin with. I'll call 911 for you. Where are you?! They'll need an address."

"NO!! PLEASE DON'T DO THAT! Not right now, anyway. And, besides, I didn't say 'burglars,' I said . . . um, 'BURGERS,' actually!!"

"DERANGED BURGERS?! Okay, dude, you need help! But NOT from the police!"

BAM! BAM! BAM!

Now the men were banging on the door of the boys' locker room across the hall! "This is INSANE!" I muttered as I cautiously peeked out. . . .

THE BURGLARS, TRYING TO
GET ME TO OPEN THE DOOR
TO THE BOYS' LOCKER ROOM!

"YEAH, KID! YOU CAN RUN, BUT YOU CAN'T HIDE! WE'RE A LOT SMARTER THAN YOU! SO JUST GIVE UP!" Tucker yelled.

Moose squealed like a pig, "CINDERELLA, OPEN THE DOOR! I'VE GOT YOUR SHOE! DON'T YOU WANT YOUR SHOE, CINDERELLA?!"

"THAT'S IT! WE'RE DONE PLAYING GAMES, YOU LITTLE PUNK!" Ralph growled. "BEFORE THIS NIGHT IS OVER, SCHOOL IS GONNA BE OUT FOR YOU, KID! PERMANENTLY!!"

"Listen, I don't mean to get into your business," the girl said, "but it sounds to me like you're in SERIOUS trouble. Are you still at SCHOOL this late? WHY . . . ?! HOW . . . ?!"

"Um . . . would you believe by . . . accident?" I muttered.

"Accident?! Wait a minute! OMG! Is this MAX CRUMBLY?! This is ERIN!"

"E-ERIN?!" I stammered. "What's up? I remember

you saying you were looking for something, but I didn't know it was your phone. Well, I . . . um, found it for you. . . ."

BAM! BAM! BAM!

"OPEN UP, KID! WE'LL BREAK THIS DOOR DOWN IF WE HAVE TO!" Ralph yelled.

"So you ARE dealing with BURGLARS! I can hear them yelling and making all that noise in the background. Please, just tell the truth!" Erin said.

"Oh! You mean . . . THOSE burglars?!" I laughed nervously. "I think I was a little harsh to call them deranged. We just got off on the wrong foot, that's all! But don't worry, I have everything under control."

"Do you actually expect me to believe that?!"

"Gee, Erin! I'd love to chat with you longer, but, unfortunately, I'm going to have to rudely hang up on you again! GOOD-BYE!"

I quickly shoved the phone back into my pocket.

Then I stared at the unlocked door.

There was no way I was going to be able to SNEAK past those three thugs.

My situation was hopeless. I was trapped.

"JUST GREAT!! I'm NEVER going to get out of here ALIVE!" I muttered aloud.

"Um, you know I'm STILL here, right?" Erin said drily.

OOPS! I guess I'd forgotten to hit the red "end call" button.

"MAX, JUST STAY ON THE LINE! I'M GOING TO CALL THE POLICE! RIGHT NOW!"

27. A FEW FRIES SHORT OF A HAPPY MEAL?! REALLY?!

The first thing the police were going to do was contact my parents. Then I'd have to explain WHERE I'd been all evening, HOW I got stuck inside my locker, WHO did it, and WHY my dad's comic book was at school.

Very soon I was going to be the ONLY eighth grader in the ENTIRE WORLD drinking juice from a sippy cup and having naptime on a fuzzy rug while being HOMESCHOOLED by my GRANDMOTHER!

Sorry, but Max C. was NOT going down like that!! Desperate times called for desperate measures, like maybe the . . . TRUTH!!

"Wait, Erin! PLEASE! Don't call the police!" I pleaded. "I'll be honest with you, okay? Those burglars have something extremely valuable that belongs to my dad. I was stupid and brought it to school after he told me not to. Do you have any idea how much trouble I'm going to be in?! And, to make matters worse, my parents will pull me out of this school.

I was just starting to like this place. Well, except for Thug Thurston! And the fact that I don't have a single friend here. I'm also sick and tired of being slammed INSIDE my locker. Okay, actually . . . I HATE THIS STUPID SCHOOL! But I HATE being homeschooled by my GRANDMA even more! And if I have to leave, at least I want to do it on my own terms. . . ."

Yes, I KNOW! I sounded pretty PATHETIC. But I had to convince Erin NOT to call the police, or my life was pretty much OVER! I continued. . . .

"Anyway, my plan is to get back my dad's property BEFORE the police get involved. All I need is fifteen minutes. Maybe even LESS time than that! Will you please just give me a chance? TRUST me on this."

Suddenly it was super quiet on the other end of the line. Had Erin hung up on me? "Hello! Are you still there? No? Actually, I don't blame you. I wouldn't waste time talking to ME either . . . ," I mumbled.

Then I heard a deep sigh.

"MAX CRUMBLY! You've given me ZERO good reasons to trust you so far! You're reckless and completely out of touch with reality. Frankly, I suspect you're a few fries short of a Happy Meal!"

OUCH!! That HURT!!

"But . . . I'm going to trust you. Just because you're my friend," she explained.

WHOA!! Did Erin Madison just call me a FRIEND?!

"But ONLY under TWO CONDITIONS!" Erin said. "First, you have to let me help you. I can use the school's new system for controlling the cameras and lights and stuff remotely to track the burglars. Then at least we can see and hear them."

"Hold on! Are you saying our school has surveillance cameras?!" I gasped in shock. "NO WAY!"

I cringed at the thought of kids laughing at videos of my numerous meltdowns and super-embarrassing antics on their phones during lunch on Tuesday. . . .

EVERYONE IN THE CAFETERIA LAUGHING AT THE CRAZY VIDEO OF ME!

"Well, it's not up and running for the entire school yet. They're installing it in phases as the PTA raises the money," Erin explained. "But it will be better than nothing. We'll have audio and video, and I'll be able to control the lights and the PA system and other stuff. I just need the password to get access."

"Oh, is that all you need? Just the password! Sounds simple enough!" I said sarcastically.

"Well, Mr. Smarty-Pants, as the president of the computer club, I had to go to the office to get the password for our website. I actually watched the principal go into his office and get it from an index card that was taped to the bottom of his bowling trophy. I'm guessing all of his passwords are written there. Do you think you can get your hands on it?"

"Seriously? A bowling trophy?! Consider it done!" I answered.

"Now, my second condition," Erin continued, "is really important. . . . DON'T YOU DARE HANG UP

ON ME AGAIN!! Put the phone on vibrate. And if you don't answer by the third ring, I'm going to assume you're in big trouble and call the cops! DEAL?!"

"Come on! I just explained all of that!" I protested.

"It's your choice, Max! Take it or leave it!"

"My, aren't WE a little BOSSY?!" I shot back.

"YEP! Twenty-four/seven! My favorite song is 'Girls Rule!! Boys Drool!!' I'm sure you've heard that one before?"

"Yes, I have. But NOT nearly as much as that CRUDDY song 'LEGO LUV'! Sorry, Erin! I'd rather listen to a toilet flush than your ringtone! But . . . yeah, it's a DEAL," I reluctantly agreed. Like I really had a choice in the matter.

"And, Max . . . one last thing . . . ," Erin said hesitantly.

"But you just said there were only TWO conditions."

"Please STAY SAFE! Or I swear! I'll come down there and . . . KILL YOU myself!! Got that?! UH-OH! I think my parents are back from their movie. E-mail me that password ASAP! I'll call you back in ten minutes, okay?"

CLICK!! Erin hung up on me before I could even answer.

As I placed the phone on vibrate and stuck it in my back pocket, I suddenly realized I was now more TERRIFIED of girls than EVER. And ONE in particular.

Erin Madison was so SMART, she was SCARY!

Suddenly I had a brilliant idea. I quickly searched the room. Just as I had suspected, there was a VENT above the lockers in the back of the room.

WOO-HOO! I felt like doing my victory dance!

I had barely climbed back inside the ventilation system when Moose, Tucker, and Ralph burst into the girls' locker room like crazed MANIACS. . . .

I JUST BARELY ESCAPED THE BURGLARS!

"I SWEAR I heard something in here!" Tucker exclaimed. "Voices AND music! Moose thought it was coming from the boys' locker room, but it sounded to me like it was coming from over here."

Ralph glared at Tucker. "Why am I NOT surprised you're hearing things?! You must have FORGOTTEN to take your MEDS again!"

"I'm NOT crazy, Ralph! I know what I heard! It was my favorite tune. You know, the one by that boy band that goes like this: 'Listen, gurl, we have a connection! I luv u more than my Lego collection!'" Tucker sang, very off-key.

"STOP SINGING! YOU'RE MAKING MY EARS BLEED!" Ralph yelled.

Suddenly Moose looked super anxious. "Listen up, guys. Maybe there are GHOSTS in this school! I saw a TV documentary on ghosts, and some of them are . . . REAL! I'm thinking we should just leave. . . ."

Ralph got SO mad, his eyes were practically bulging out of his head.

"I HOPE they're REAL!! You know WHY? Because I'd FIRE you two IDIOTS and HIRE the GHOSTS!! Then I could finally get down to business, LOAD UP THE STINKIN' COMPUTERS, AND MOVE ON WITH MY DANG LIFE! TUCKER! MOOSE! THERE'S NOTHING IN THIS ROOM! NOTHING!! NO VOICES! NO MUSIC! NO GHOSTS! DO YOU UNDERSTAND ME?!"

"Yeah, boss," Tucker and Moose answered glumly.

Just then Ralph's cell phone rang. He looked at it and cringed.

"SHEESH! It's TINA again?! She's going NUTS! How am I supposed to get any work done with her calling me every five minutes, screaming at me about her mother?! Just forget the kid. He's probably harmless anyway. Let's load up the computers and get the heck out of here. Before TINA has a COW!!"

"Listen, boss, since we're not gonna be wasting any

more time looking for that kid, can we at least EAT our PIZZA now? It's getting cold!" Moose whined.

"Yeah!" Tucker agreed. "The buffalo wings are getting cold too!"

"NOOO!!" Ralph bellowed. "What part of 'NO' do you FOOLS not understand?!"

Moose glared at Ralph. "Well, Aunt Tina is going to be VERY upset when she finds out you wouldn't let her favorite nephews eat dinner!"

Tucker crossed his arms and smirked at Ralph. "Yeah! And Aunt Tina is already REALLY, REALLY mad at you!"

All the color drained right out of Ralph's face. He looked like he was about to have a stroke!

Honestly! If stupidity were a crime, these guys would be sentenced to LIFE in prison!! Tucker, Ralph, and Moose didn't know it yet, but if things went according to plan, TINA and COLD PIZZA were going to be the LEAST of their problems!

28. HOW I DISCOVERED
THE STICKY NOTE OF DOOM

I was happy that Erin agreed to help me out. I guess this meant we were FRIENDS again.

CRAZY, right?!

Maybe I'll join the computer club after all and we can hang out after school.

But don't get it twisted!

Like I said earlier, I'm NOT crushing on her or anything. I hardly even know the girl.

And yes, I really needed to break the news to her that, in addition to her cell phone, I was ALSO borrowing her _Ice Princess_ costume.

But since she was so traumatized by her play getting canceled, I'd probably just keep the costume a SECRET for a little while longer.

I know. I KNOW! You DON'T have to tell me.

Okay, people, let's say it all together. . . .

DUDE! THAT'S JUST WRONG ON SO MANY LEVELS!

Anyway, I guess I gave the burglars such a hard time, they'd FINALLY given up on trying to capture me.

I was a little INSULTED that they actually called me HARMLESS. Really?

~~What am I?~~ ~~CHOPPED LIVER?!~~

I may not be as MEAN as Ralph, as STRONG as Moose, or as blissfully STUPID as Tucker.

But I DID have a private entrance into the ventilation system from my locker, which gave me SECRET access to the ENTIRE SCHOOL!

I COULD TOTALLY RUN THIS PLACE! FOR REAL!

My plan was to spy on the burglars and watch their every move until I got the perfect opportunity to swoop in and swipe my dad's comic book.

Then I'd dial 911 for the police and call it a night.

The good news was that my new clothing made it a lot easier to move around inside the vents.

But crawling around on my hands and knees was getting old.

What I needed was . . .

SPEED!!

I was passing by the vent door to the janitor's closet and just happened to look inside.

That's when I spotted the PERFECT piece of equipment. . . .

IT WAS KIND OF A SOUPED-UP, OVERSIZED SKATEBOARD!

It had four-inch nonskid wheels that were soft, rubbery, and completely quiet, and, most important, it was . . .

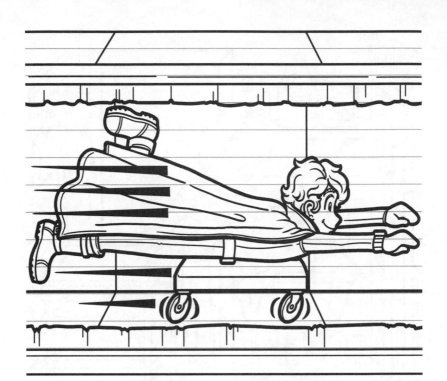

SUPER FAST!!!

Now I could get from one end of the school to the other in LESS than sixty seconds....

ZOOOOOM!!!

I was rocketing through those vents SO fast that it almost seemed like I was actually...

FLYING!!!

It was the COOLEST thing EVER!

I felt like a real TEEN SUPERHERO!

I was fighting EVIL and INJUSTICE in the DANK, DARK, and sometimes DANGEROUS halls of MIDDLE SCHOOL!!

Things were going to be different in my life from this point forward.

Starting with my LOCKER!

I removed my combination lock and reattached it UNDER my door handle with a paper clip so that it only appeared to be locked.

Since I could now open the door from the inside, I would NEVER, EVER be locked in there AGAIN!!

~~SORRY ABOUT THAT, THUG!~~

~~GET OVER IT!~~

I did my VICTORY DANCE and moonwalked down the hallway back to the vent.

My next task was to get that password for Erin.

Which, unfortunately, meant SNOOPING around inside . . .

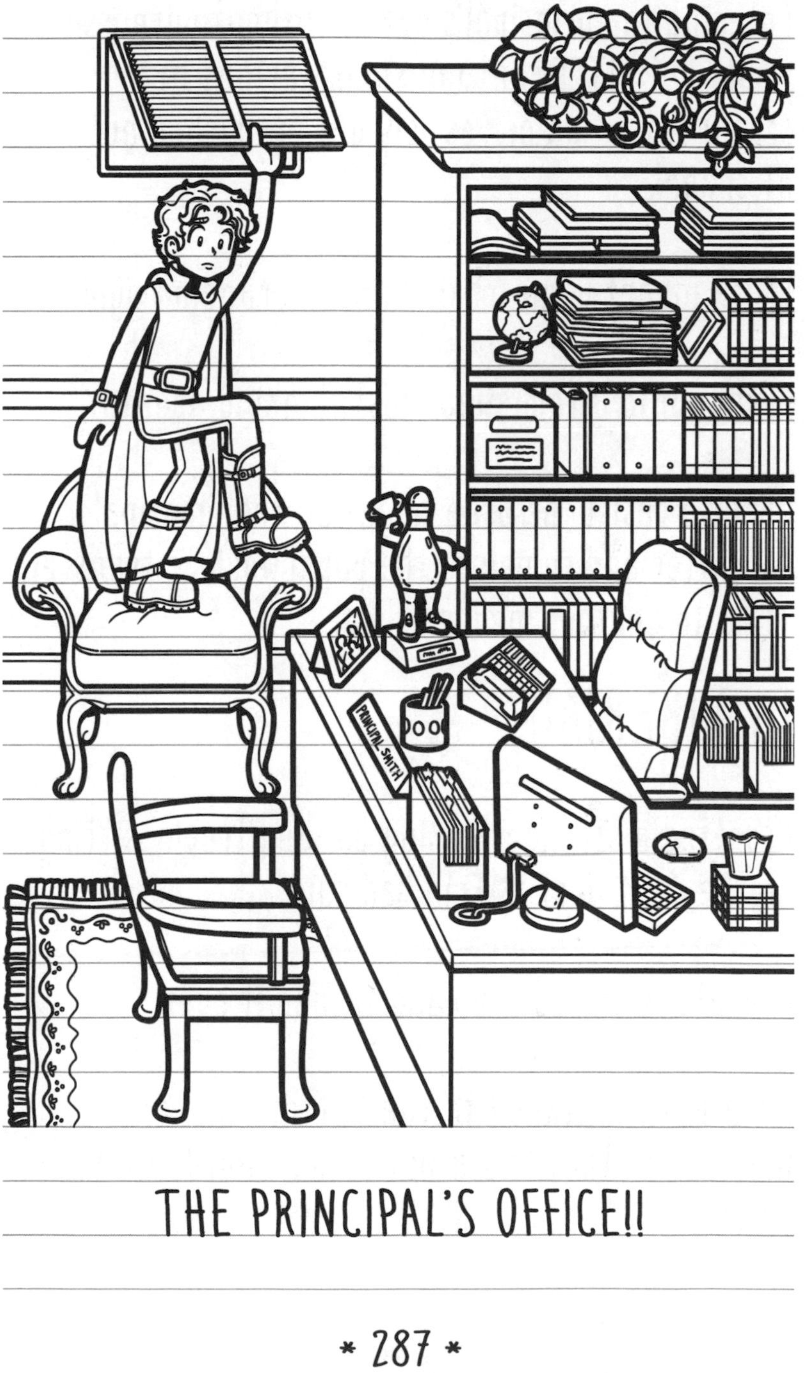
PRINCIPAL SMITH

THE PRINCIPAL'S OFFICE!!

Entering the principal's office without permission would DEFINITELY get me some serious after-school detention or possibly get me kicked out of school.

Which meant homeschooling with Grandma again.

I broke into a cold sweat just thinking about it.

I had to resist the urge to get on the principal's computer and complete the paperwork to transfer THUG to another middle school.

In SIBERIA!!

I spotted a strange-looking bowling trophy sitting on the desk, just as Erin had said.

I carefully picked it up and turned it over.

Sure enough, taped to the bottom was an index card that had a list of passwords written on it! . . .

MISSION ACCOMPLISHED!

I took a picture of the index card with Erin's cell phone. Then I pulled up her e-mail address and sent her a copy of the photo.

I had placed the index card back under the trophy and was about to leave when I noticed several yellow sticky notes stuck on the computer monitor.

Unfortunately, one of them was about ME! . . .

TO: Principal Smith
FROM: Kathy W.
RE: MAXWELL CRUMBLY, 8th grade

Max was tardy twice today, missed a math quiz, and seemed upset about something. His parents asked to be updated about any issues.

Maybe give them a call on Tuesday to set up a meeting!

ISSUES?! What issues?! I DON'T have any STINKIN' issues!!

I'd managed to SURVIVE Thug and three criminals! And now my PRINCIPAL was going to WRECK everything by meeting with my PARENTS?!

GIVE ME A BREAK!

I stared at the note. What if it just disappeared into thin air? He'd probably never even miss it.

Yes, I know! Taking stuff that didn't belong to me was dishonest and would RUIN my life.

~~Although, being homeschooled and eating animal crackers until I VOMITED would pretty much RUIN it too.~~

I SNATCHED the note, balled it up, and stuck it in my pocket.

Then I ran, jumped on the chair, bounced off the seat cushion, and dove inside the vent, just like a ninja.

SORRY, Principal Smith!

But Max C. wasn't going down like that!

29. THE MORTIFYING MISADVENTURE OF MAX CRUMBLY!! (SORRY, DUDES! MY BAD!)

Erin must have gotten her hands on another cell phone, because I just got a text from her. . . .

> Thanks 4 the password ☺. Remote access granted!
>
> Call you in 2 minutes.

I needed to find a secluded place as far away as possible from the computer lab so I could talk to her without being overheard.

Someplace like, maybe . . . THE BOILER ROOM!!

It was on the far west side of the school, so I took off speeding through the vents as fast as I could go. I needed to make a left, two rights, and then a left. Or was it a right, two lefts, and then a right? I wasn't really sure, but I wasn't all that worried.

Hey! What could possibly go wrong when you're blasting like a rocket through an enclosed vent?!! . . .

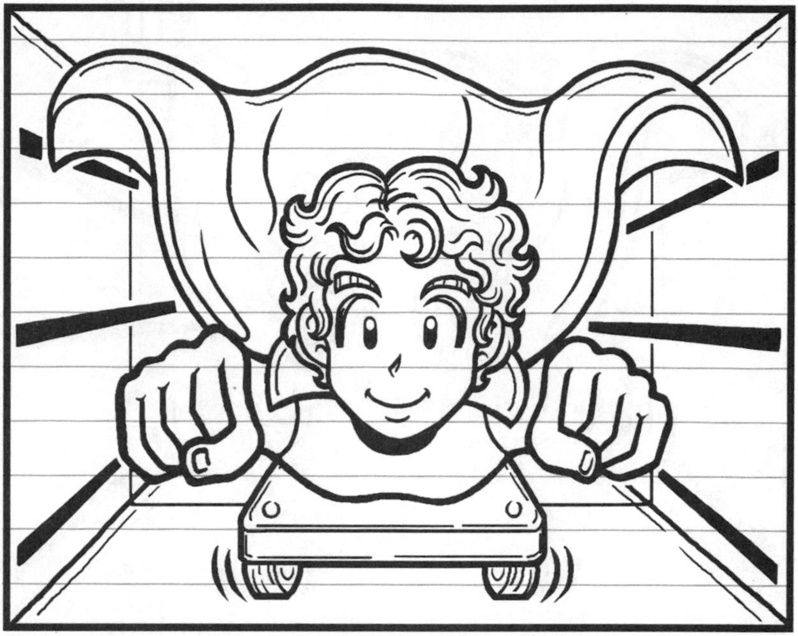

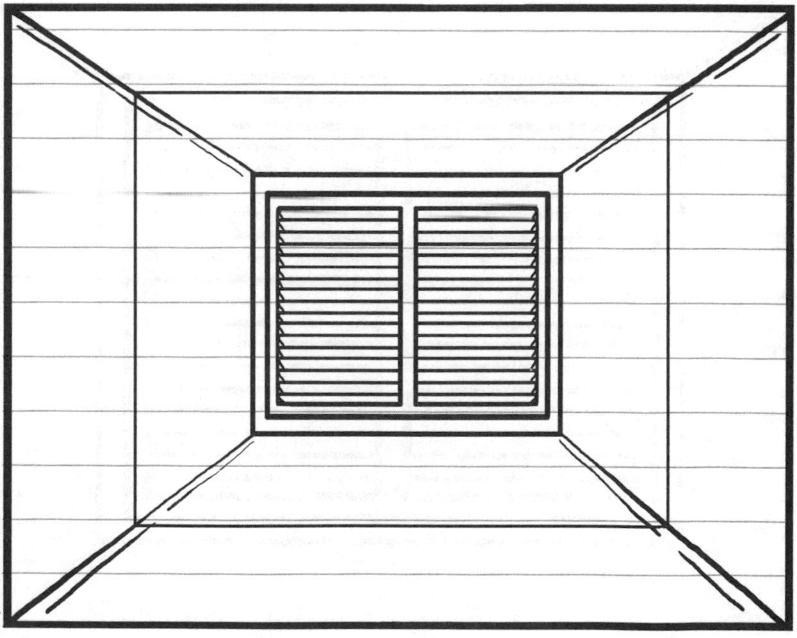

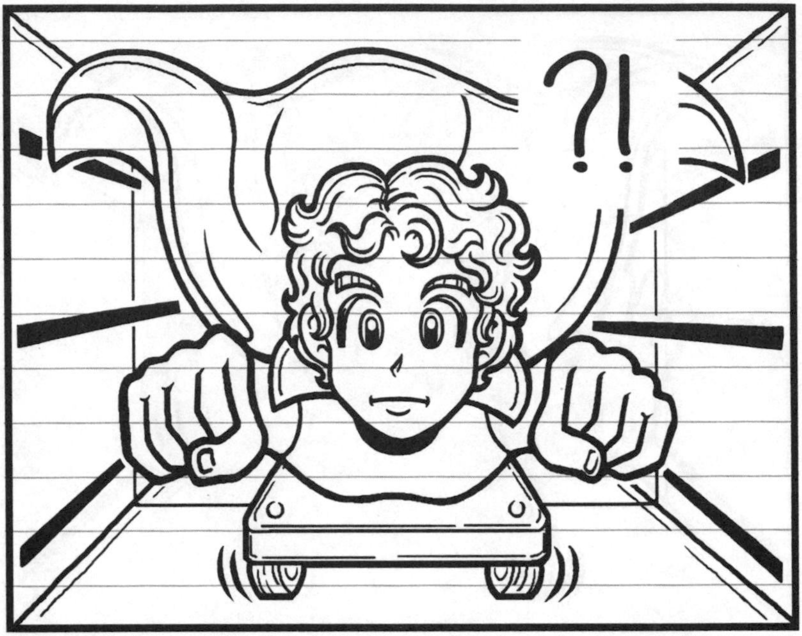
?!

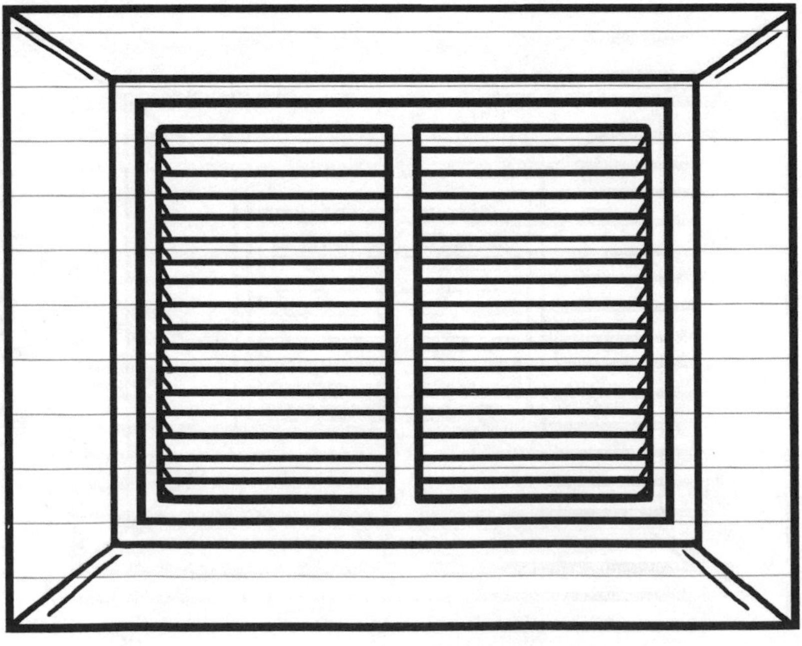

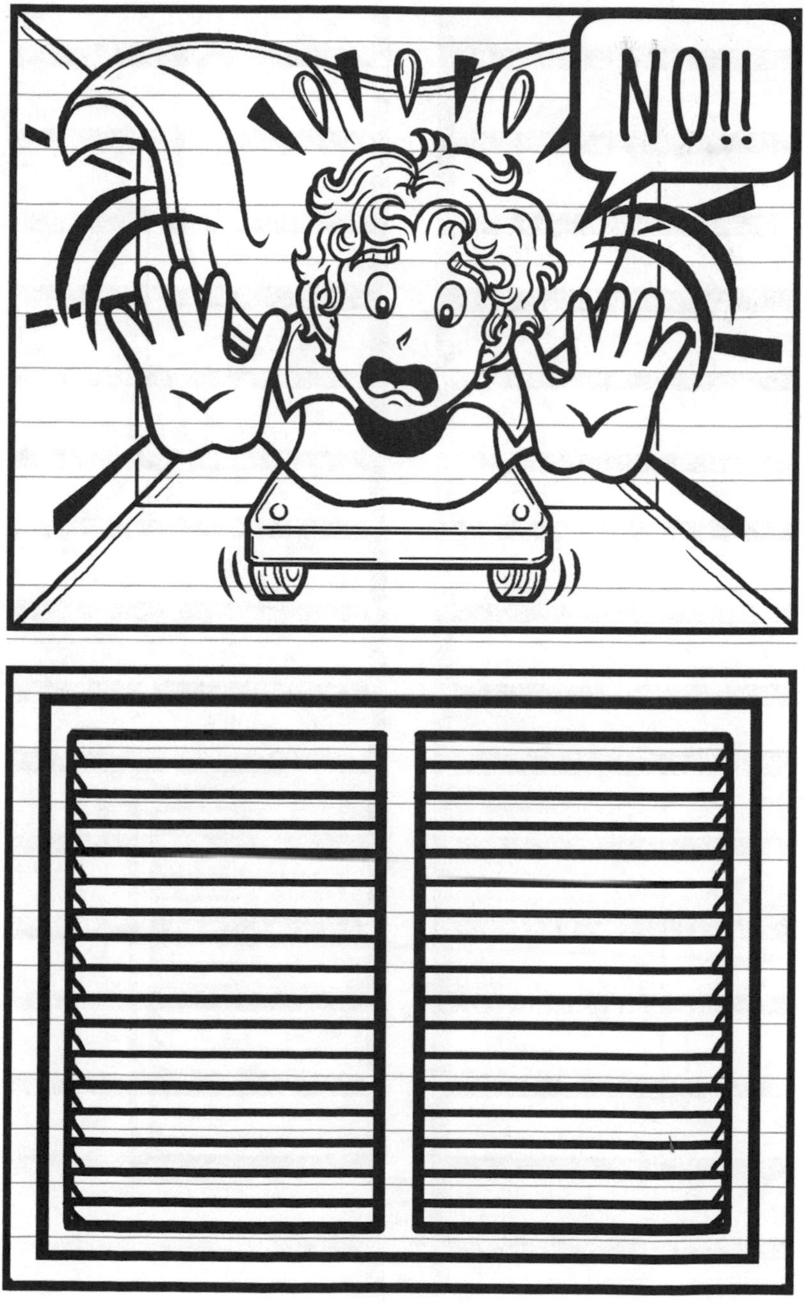
NO!!

[redacted]

[redacted]

[redacted]

[redacted]

[redacted]

[redacted]

[redacted]

[redacted]

[redacted]

[redacted]

[redacted]

[redacted]

[redacted]

[redacted]

[redacted]

[redacted]

[redacted]

[redacted]

[redacted]

[redacted]

[redacted]

[redacted]

[redacted]

[redacted]

[redacted]

[redacted]

[redacted]

[redacted]

[redacted]

[redacted]

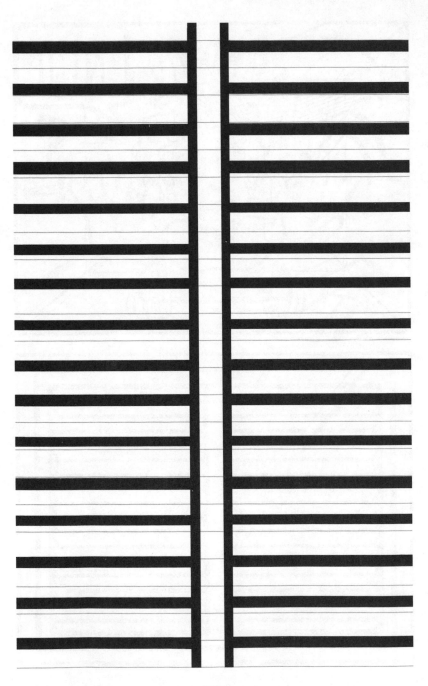

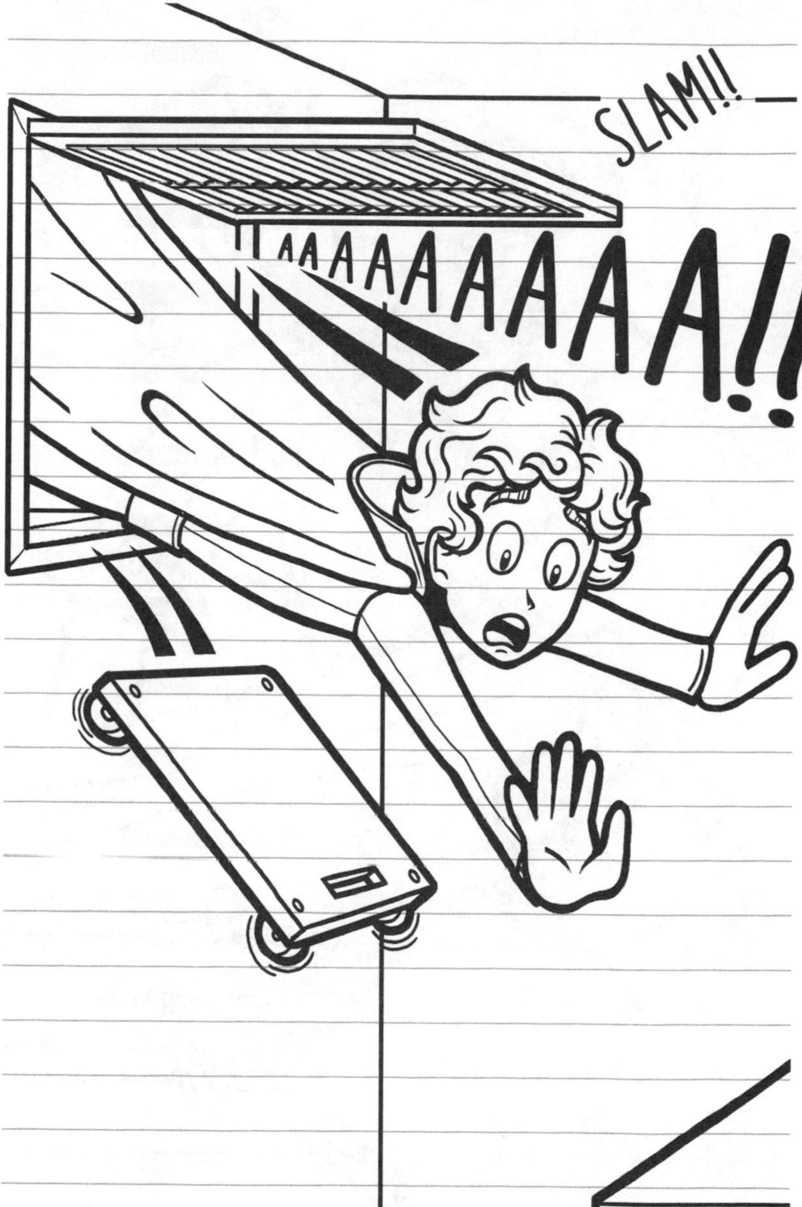
SLAM!!
AAAAAAAAAAA!!

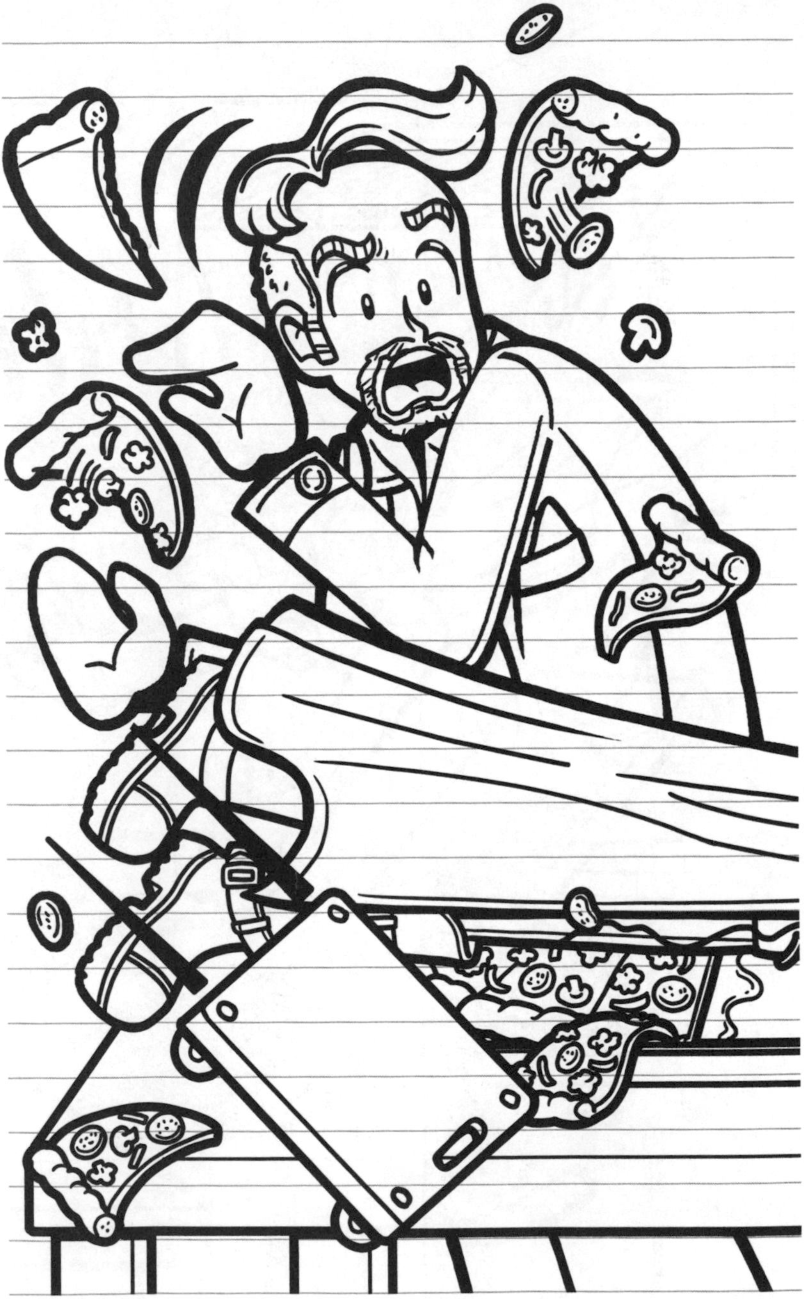

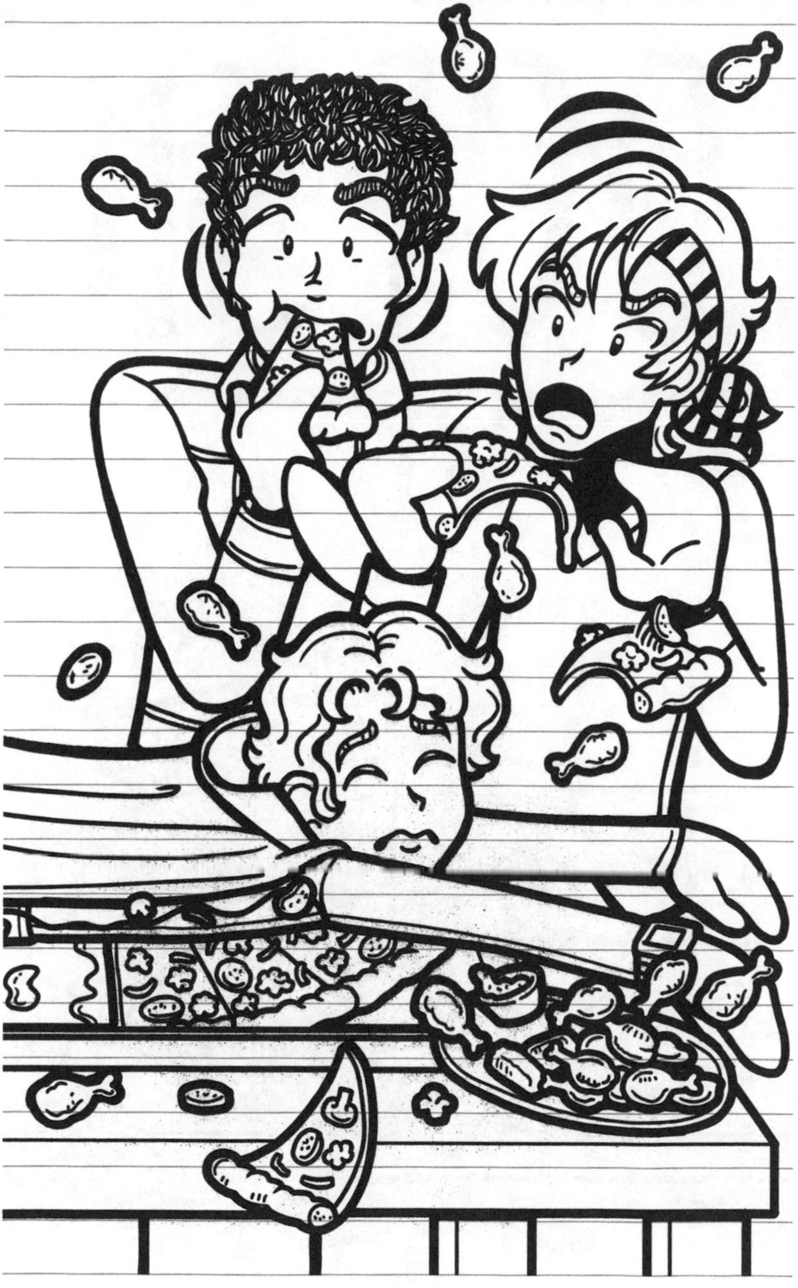

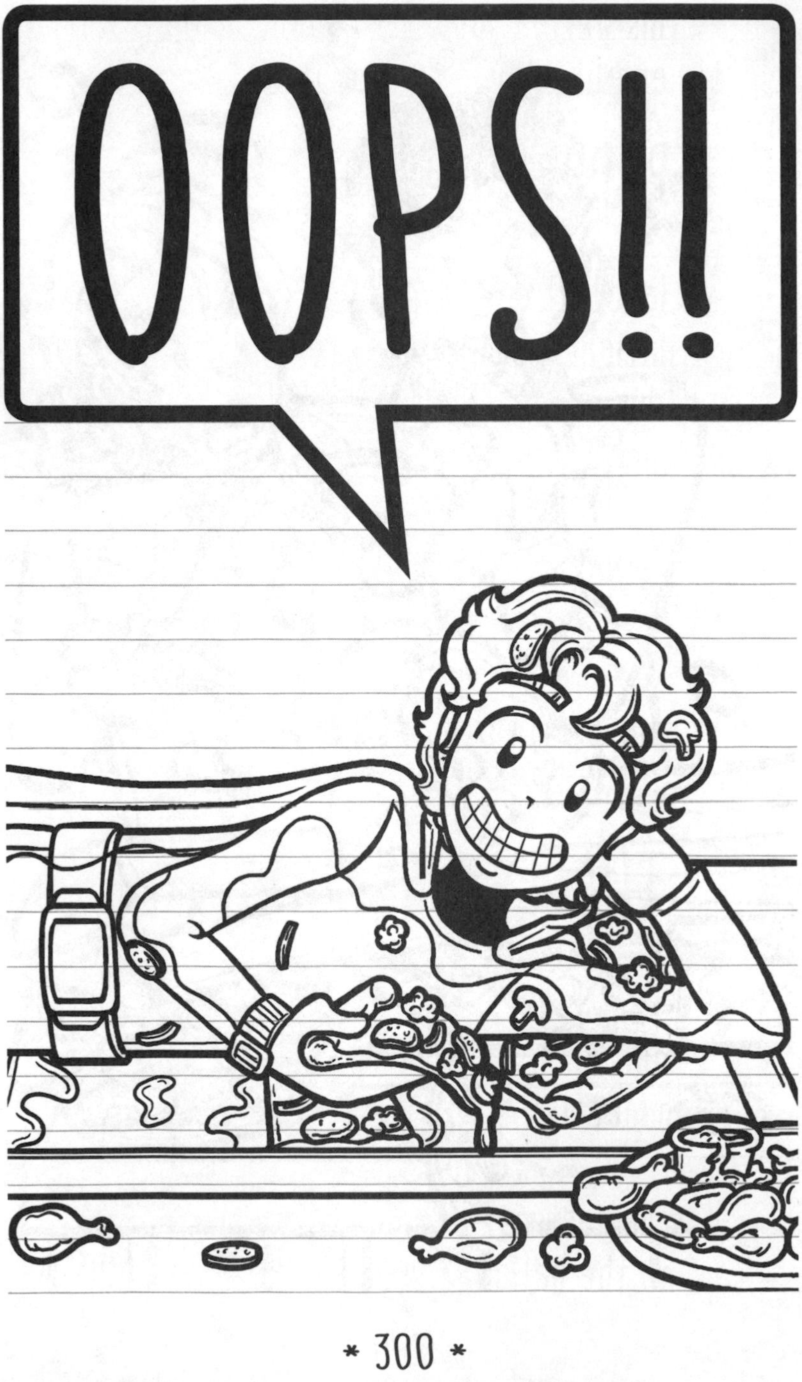
OOPS!!

Okay, if this were a superhero comic book, it would probably end like this:

HOLY PEPPERONI!

When we last left our hero, he'd crashed through the ventilation system at ninety miles per hour, surprised his evil archnemeses, and totally RUINED their dinner!

Is this the FINAL misadventure of our hero, Max Crumbly?!

Can the computer whiz ERIN help him out of this colossal ~~HOT and CHEESY~~ MESS?!

~~Is he ACTUALLY going to EAT that slice of PIZZA?!!~~

Will our courageous hero make it out of South Ridge Middle School ALIVE?!

Or will he be destroyed like a greasy piece of sausage on the half-baked PIZZA CRUST of DOOM?

I bet you can't believe I'm leaving you hanging, just like they do in my favorite comic books! Sorry, but all I can say at this point is . . .

TO BE CONTINUED!!

Now you know a little about me and my crazy life. Hey, I WISH I was making this stuff up!

I still haven't quite figured out if it's HARDER to be a SUPERHERO or a mild-mannered, socially challenged, awkward middle school student ~~known as BARF!~~

~~YES! I KNOW I totally MESSED UP! I'm STILL trying to get the HANG of all of this SUPERHERO stuff, okay?~~

~~GIVE ME A BREAK! It's definitely NOT as easy as it looks!~~

But what I DO know is that I'm going to try to become the AWESOME HERO I've always wanted to be.

And if I can do it . . . YOU can TOO!

For MORE Max,
be sure to read BOOK TWO:

the
misadventures
of MAX
CRUMBLY

MIDDLE SCHOOL MAYHEM

ACKNOWLEDGMENTS

I can't believe that Max Crumbly has FINALLY arrived to save the day!

Let's start with my superhero team, led by the incredible Batgirl herself, my editorial director, Liesa Abrams Mignogna. I'm thrilled to venture with you into the superhero world, one you know so well. Thank you for sharing your exceptional creative talent as I found my new voice. When malevolent deadlines reared their ugly heads, you pulverized them, and for this I am grateful. Thank you for your endless passion and enthusiasm. Yes, this is all in a day's work for the bat caped crusader. And Bat Baby helped!

Karin Paprocki, my ingenious art director, who uses her powerful design brilliance to create thrilling covers and exciting layouts. Lesser beings would have succumbed to the pressures of the unknown, but you prevailed. No devious artwork got past your eagle eye. Thank you for working tirelessly to ensure that all Max C. illustrations were awesome.

My managing editor, Katherine Devendorf, who kept everything in perfect alignment and harmony even under the most vicious deadlines. Your command over words makes you a formidable foe to any villainous sentence structure. Thank you for being a brave editorial defender.

Daniel Lazar, my phenomenal, hardworking superagent at Writers House, with telepathic powers and superior intellect. Your uncanny ability to know what I'm thinking and to think outside the box makes working with you a dream. Your literary agent instincts are unrivaled in this universe. Thank you for being my friend, confidant, and courageous supporter.

To my league of superheroes at Aladdin/ Simon & Schuster, Mara Anastas, Mary Marotta, Jon Anderson, Julie Doebler, Jennifer Romanello, Faye Bi, Carolyn Swerdloff, Tara Grieco, Lucille Rettino, Matt Pantoliano, Michelle Leo, Candace McManus, Anthony Parisi, Sarah McCabe, Emma Sector, Christina Solazzo, Lauren Forte, Christine Marshall, Crystal Velasquez, Christina Pecorale, Gary Urda, and the entire sales force. You each possess rare powers and abilities to generate supersonic sales and create innovative marketing campaigns. Thanks for your hard work and commitment. You are truly the best team in the publishing universe and a force to be reckoned with.

A special thanks to Torie Doherty-Munro at Writers House; my foreign rights agents Maja Nikolic, Cecilia de la Campa, Angharad Kowal, and James Munro; and Zoé, Marie, and Joy—you are an elite group of crusaders with supernatural abilities. Thanks for being a part of our team.

To Erin, my super-talented coauthor; Nikki, my super-talented illustrator; Kim, my manager (and trusty sidekick); Doris; Don; and my entire family—YOU are my HEROES! With your wisdom, unwavering support, and love, you have made my wildest dreams come true. Thank you for believing in me. Max Crumbly today! And tomorrow . . . the WORLD!

RACHEL RENÉE RUSSELL

is the #1 *New York Times* bestselling author of the blockbuster book series Dork Diaries and the exciting new series The Misadventures of Max Crumbly.

There are more than twenty-five million copies of her books in print worldwide, and they have been translated into thirty-six languages.

She enjoys working with her two daughters, Erin and Nikki, who help write and illustrate her books.

Rachel's message is "Become the hero you've always admired!"

Don't miss more diaries

Rachel Renée Russell
DORK diaries
Tales from a NOT-SO-Fabulous Life

Rachel Renée Russell
DORK diaries
Tales from a NOT-SO-Popular Party Girl

Rachel Renée Russell
DORK diaries
Tales from a NOT-SO-Talented Pop Star

Rachel Renée Russell
DORK diaries
Tales from a NOT-SO-Happy Heartbreaker

Rachel Renée Russell
DORK diaries
OMG! ALL ABOUT ME DIARY!

Rachel Renée Russell
DORK diaries
Tales from a NOT-SO-Glam TV Star

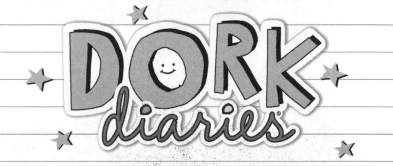

by Rachel Renée Russell!

MOST IMPORTANT TIP EVER FROM NIKKI MAXWELL:

Always let your inner **DORK** shine through!

#1 New York Times Bestselling Series